T0276942

AN
UNRESTORED
WOMAN

AN
UNRESTORED
WOMAN

Shobha Rao

FLATIRON
BOOKS
NEW YORK

This is a work of fiction. All of the characters, organizations, and events portrayed in this novel are either products of the author's imagination or are used fictitiously.

www.flatironbooks.com

The following stories have been or will be published. Previously published stories may appear in a slightly different form in this book.

"Kavitha and Mustafa," *Nimrod International Journal* (volume 58, winter 2014)
"The Imperial Police," *Wasafiri* (UK, forthcoming)
"Unleashed," *Water~Stone Review* (August 2014)
"An Unrestored Woman," *PMS poemmemoirstory* (issue 13, spring 2014)
"The Road to Mirpur Khas," *Tincture* (Australia, issue 2, winter 2013)
"The Lost Ribbon," *The Missing Slate* (Pakistan, April 2013) and *The Four Quarters Magazine* (India, August 2013)

Designed by Steven Seighman

The Library of Congress Cataloging-in-Publication Data is available upon request.

ISBN 978-1-250-07382-2 (hardcover)
ISBN 978-1-250-07383-9 (e-book)

Our books may be purchased in bulk for promotional, educational, or business use. Please contact your local bookseller or the Macmillan Corporate and Premium Sales Department at 1-800-221-7945, extension 5442, or by e-mail at MacmillanSpecialMarkets@macmillan.com.

First Edition: March 2016

For my parents, Kamala and Singiresu S. Rao, and for M

CONTENTS

Author's Note   *xi*

An Unrestored Woman   *1*
The Merchant's Mistress   *17*
The Imperial Police   *41*
Unleashed   *61*
Blindfold   *81*
The Lost Ribbon   *105*
The Opposite of Sex   *123*
Such a Mighty River   *143*
The Road to Mirpur Khas   *165*
The Memsahib   *183*
Kavitha and Mustafa   *201*
Curfew   *221*

Glossary   *239*
Acknowledgments   *243*

All I desired was to walk upon such
an earth that had no maps.
—Michael Ondaatje

Author's Note

In August 1947, the decline of the British Empire on the Indian subcontinent led to the formation of two new sovereign states: India and Pakistan. The event, commonly known as Partition, led to the establishment of Pakistan as an Islamic republic with a majority Muslim population, while India emerged as a secular state with a Hindu majority. The hastily drawn boundary between the two countries, called the Radcliffe Line, resulted in a colossal transfer of people between the two nations. Although estimates vary, it is believed that eight to ten million people were displaced from their homes and villages, with primarily Hindus, Muslims, and Sikhs seeking refuge in what they hoped would be the relative safety of the religious majority. This mass movement of people incited numerous acts of violence on both sides, with nearly a million people killed in the migratory effort. The transfer of populations between India and Pakistan is considered the largest peacetime migration in all of human history.

As with a majority of conflicts, women and children during the Partition of India and Pakistan were often the most vulnerable. The specific brutalities inflicted on women were legion, kidnappings among them. Officially, it is estimated that 50,000 Muslim women in India and 33,000 Hindu and Sikh women in Pakistan were abducted. Added to this, many who were abducted were forcibly returned to families who, in some instances, no longer wanted them, considering them impure. In 1949, India legislated the return of these women with the Abducted Persons (Recovery and Restoration) Act. Though the commonly used term for these women is *recovered* women, I have chosen to refer to them as *restored*. The distinction may seem trivial, but it is necessary, for I believe that while the recovery of a person is possible, the restoration of a human being to her original state is not.

AN UNRESTORED WOMAN

Neela, on the night she learned of her husband's death, sat under the banyan tree outside their hut and felt an intense hunger. It was on the night of the train accident. No, not an accident, she corrected herself. Not at all. She felt this same hunger on her wedding day. She was thirteen years old and she sat on the altar wearing a sparkling red sari and the gold mangal sutra around her neck—thin, even by the reduced standards of the impoverished northern village—and tried desperately to silence her growling stomach.

The hunger on her wedding day might've been caused by the tempting mountains of food stacked around her. Fruits, coconuts, laddoos, twisted piles of orange jilebi. She'd never seen so much food; her mouth watered. She hadn't eaten since early morning and that had only been a meager helping of rice and buttermilk. Neela eyed the bananas and mangoes piled on the plate between her and the priest. He was reciting Sanskrit prayers. Her new husband, who sat beside her, wiry and dark like a dry summer chili, was turned away from her, talking to a man she didn't recognize. In truth she hardly even recognized her groom. Her red veil obscured him from view. Besides, she'd only seen him once before; she'd stolen a glimpse when he'd sat talking with her father, both of them bent and pecking over the details of her marriage like two crows over a piece of stale bread.

Her father had said it was a good match; he'd given her future husband—who was twenty-four years old and owned a tea shop catering to the commuter trains between Amritsar and Lahore—two cows, a trunk full of pots and pans, a bag of seed, and a green woolen blanket. Even the thickness of the gold necklace had been negotiated. Babu, her groom, had scowled at its flimsiness and had only been appeased when Neela's father had said, "Look. Look at that girl. Strong as an ox. She'll bear you no less than ten sons!"

Neela stared at the plate. She obviously couldn't eat one of the mangoes but why not a banana? If only she could sneak it from the plate then she could manage peeling it under her veil. Her bent head would hide the chewing. She extended an arm forward surreptitiously. Then a little farther. She sighed. It was just beyond her reach. Someone would notice. She pulled back, weak, hungrier than ever. The plump yellow of the bananas called to her. Their smooth skins were the edge of a sunrise. They were the voice of her mother. She'd died giving birth to Neela but Neela had imagined her voice many, many times, flawless and brave and cool like the banana skin. Just then the priest shifted his legs and jostled the plate. What luck! It bumped closer to Neela. This was

her chance. Her arm darted out, plucked the outermost banana, and whisked it under her veil. The first bite slid down
her throat and into her empty stomach. Her eyes widened
with delight just as her husband's had when he'd opened the
trunk full of glistening pots.

The details of the train wreck trickled down to Neela. First
over the news wire, heard by the men of the village over the
transistor radio in the home of Lalla, the village elder. Neela
had once seen this famous radio—the only one among all of
the neighboring villages. The smooth wooden box with the
mysterious voices spilling out of it was placed on a high shelf
and protected from dust and insects by a velvet cloth; even
Lalla's wife was forbidden to touch it. He brought the news
to her mother-in-law, whom Lalla came to see as soon as the
news program ended, just before dinner. Neela was hungry;
she was about to set out three plates when he told her the
news. "Those ugly Muslims," he said. "They would torch a
train full of children as long as they were Hindu." Her mother-
in-law, nearly blind, kind and gentle compared to most
mother-in-laws Neela had heard stories about, had only
looked up at Lalla with her sad, unadorned eyes and said,
"Every mother will tell you: that train *was* full of children."
    The events, as Neela peeked from behind the bamboo
screen separating the main room of the hut from the kitchen,
followed many of the stories of madness in the months after
Partition. The train had been traveling its western course,
the last evening run to Lahore. Babu had gotten on with

his kettle of tea at Wagah and that was the last anyone had seen of him. The train had been ambushed a few miles outside of Wagah by a horde of Muslim men. They'd torched each of the cars one by one, back to front, as if lighting a row of candles. "My son's body," Neela's mother-in-law asked slowly. Lalla shook his head. "They were laid out like rows of roasted corn," he said indecently. "No one can tell them apart." Then he rose to leave, handing her mother-in-law something Neela couldn't see. "Enough for both of you," he said, closing the door behind him.

The next morning Neela's mother-in-law bathed, dressed in a crisp white sari (the only color she was allowed to wear as a widow), and conducted her daily prayers while Neela heated water and the few drops of milk they could afford for tea. Then she waited. She was fifteen years old. And now she too was a widow.

Her mother-in-law, bent by a long and pitiless life, entered the kitchen. She sat in her usual corner on a thin reed mat and looked at Neela. Since Partition the cataracts in her gray eyes had ripened like winter squash, burrowing into the hollows of her wrinkled brown face. They brimmed now with tears. "My child," she whispered. Neela couldn't tell if she was referring to Neela or to some memory of her son. Then her mother-in-law reached up and brushed at Neela's face. The gesture was blunt, nearly cruel, but she managed to wipe the kumkum from Neela's forehead. The crimson powder drifted down and a few specks landed in Neela's cup. They floated on the surface like tiny red islands on a dirty sea.

"Finish your tea, beti," her mother-in-law said. "Then we'll take care of your hair." Neela nodded. She would soon be bald. She would never again be allowed to use kumkum or anything else to adorn her face. She would not be allowed to grow out her hair or go to the temple or to ever wear anything but white, the color of death. Even the thin gold mangal sutra she slid off her neck and handed to her mother-in-law, who buried it deep in the bag of rice for safekeeping. Though none of this Neela minded, not very much, not as much as she'd minded the nights with Babu.

They hadn't been so bad in the beginning. He'd seemed just as shy as she was when he'd reached for her in the dark. There had been blood and a little pain but that had soon passed. It was only after a few months that Babu had become rough. Tugging at her sari, pushing himself inside her, slapping her if she resisted. She knew it was her duty, a part of being an obedient wife, and she bore it without a word of complaint. But what she didn't understand was why he never spoke to her. Why he ate his dinner without a word. Even when the jasmine bloomed lush and fragrant in her hair, and she served him tea in the evening shade of the banyan tree, he'd hardly look at her.

"Will you build me a swing?" she'd once asked, a year after they'd been married. "It could hang from there," she'd said, pointing to the lowest branch of the tree.

He'd looked up toward where she was pointing, into the wide cover of green, leathery leaves and hoary branches and said, "Swinging is for monkeys. Are you a monkey?"

Neela thought of monkeys and of bananas and realized—with a clarity that was surprising in its force—that she recognized the man sitting in front of her no more than she had on their wedding day.

On some afternoons, while her mother-in-law slept through the heat of midday, Neela cried from loneliness and dread. Night was drawing close. And she missed her playmates, most of whom were now married. She also missed her father but knew that when he'd kissed her on the forehead after the wedding the tears in his eyes had not just been from sadness but from relief: he'd married off his last daughter. In the midst of her tears Neela sometimes found herself peering down at her stomach, willing it to grow; at least then she'd have someone to talk to. Someone to hold.

By the time the puja was conducted and Neela's hair lay in a pile, coiled like seething black serpents on the dirt floor of the hut, it was early evening. The leaves hung dusty and exhausted on the banyan tree. The sun hissed and spit as it neared the horizon. Neela was watching it from the doorway when her mother-in-law ushered her inside. A pair of Babu's pants, hung from a nail beside the door, brushed against her newly shorn scalp and made it tingle. Neela thought of an army of ants scampering across her head and smiled.

Her mother-in-law looked at her. Her hand trembled as it reached for Neela's. How different they were: Neela's moist and smooth, her mother-in-law's tough and wrinkled like dried dates. She was crying again. "We'll drink this tonight," she said, slipping a thick bottle into Neela's hand. The bottle was made of dark brown glass—the color of a piece of chocolate she'd once eaten as a child, given to her by a wealthy uncle who was a clerk in a dry goods shop—and filled with liquid. "What is it?" Neela asked.

"Something to make us sleep," her mother-in-law said.

And Neela understood. Her father-in-law had died years ago, she'd never even met him, and now Babu was dead. What good were two women, two widows, alone in this world?

"Lalla said it would be quiet, peaceful, like falling asleep in a mother's arms," she said. Neela bent her head and wondered what that might feel like, to fall asleep in a mother's arms.

Neela woke the second morning after her husband's death with a pounding headache. She was groggy; her muscles ached. She was confused. Her mother-in-law had drunk half the bottle then handed it to Neela. She'd sipped it, not more than a drop or two, and held it in her mouth. Neela had waited till the old woman had closed her eyes then run to the back of the hut and vomited. She'd then slipped into the kitchen and buried the bottle in the bag of rice. Now, in the grim morning light, she turned to look at her mother-in-law.

Her chest was still. Neela reached for her then snapped her hand away. Her mother-in-law's body was cold. Her eyes were open and lifeless, staring in the direction of the banyan tree.

Lalla came by later in the morning. He did nothing to hide his disgust. "You fool," he scowled. "You think that bottle was cheap? You spit it out, didn't you?" He eyed her with a cold stare. Neela wrapped her palloo tighter around her shoulders. "No," she said, "I didn't spit it out." Her face grew warm. What if he asked to see the bottle?

"Give me your mangal sutra," he finally said. "I'll see what I can do." Neela went to the bag of rice and dug her fingers into the kernels. How pleasant: the cool of the rice. Her hand first grazed the solidness of the bottle. She kept her expression unchanged; Lalla was watching her. She wriggled past it until she found the necklace. When her hands came up they were coated in a thin dust as if hundreds of butterfly wings had brushed against them. She handed Lalla the necklace. He returned an hour later and told her he'd secured passage for her on a bus headed for a nearby camp. It was set up by the Indian government, he said.

"For what?" she asked.

"For items that are useless," he said. "Like you."

When the bus pulled into the camp, some four hours after it'd set off from Attari, Neela noticed the small handwritten sign posted on the gate: CAMP FOR REFUGEES AND UN-RESTORED WOMEN. District 15, East Punjab. Beyond was a row of tents. She was assigned to a small, dirty cot in the largest of the tents. Neela set down her bag, containing only her mother-in-law's white sari so that she'd have a change of clothes, and a pair of socks and chappals for when it got too cold to go barefoot. She looked around the enclosure. It was filled with women, all wearing white and all of them bald. It was funny, the rows and rows of shiny heads, and Neela smiled despite knowing that all of them, including herself, were supposed to be in mourning.

She met Renu on the first night. She was Neela's age, maybe a year or two older. Her wide eyes were lustrous and pretty even under her shorn head. She was as thin as a reed and Neela realized they'd been assigned to the same cot due to lack of space. Renu took one look at Neela and burst out laughing. "Do you know you have the silliest bump on the top of your head?" she asked. Neela shook her head. "Haven't you looked in a mirror since your head was shaved?" Neela shook her head again. "It looks like a hillock in my old village," Renu said. "The one our temple is built on." She pulled a handkerchief from her bag, knotted it into a wide dome, and balanced it on Neela's head. "There," she said. "Now you have the temple too."

They were inseparable after that. They ate together, did chores together, gossiped together. They played among the tents and fetched water from the nearby well in the mornings. Sometimes they slept holding hands. Renu told her about her husband. He'd been a farmer. They'd had three acres and a pair of goats. The Muslim mob had burned everything, including her husband. Renu said this with tears in her eyes and Neela knew she should feel sad for her but she didn't. She did feel awful that her husband had died but she was also glad that he had; how else would they have met?

During their fifth night in the camp Renu and Neela lay on their cot talking in whispers. Since the camp had no electricity or kerosene they slept soon after their dinner of one thin roti and a small spoonful of potato curry. Most of the other women were already asleep. Renu had snuck in an extra roti for Neela, and she nibbled it while Renu talked about their lives.

"What will we do?" she asked.

"We could cook," Neela said, taking a bite of the roti. "And clean. My sisters do that for rich families in Amritsar."

"But we're just villagers." Renu breathed. "Who'll hire us?"

"I'll take care of you," Neela said, thinking of the gold mangal sutra she'd handed over to Lalla.

There was silence. Renu sighed. "It wasn't the actual, you know, *chum chum* that was nice. It was how he held me afterward."

Neela stopped chewing.

Renu looked at her in the dark. "Didn't yours?"

"No."

"Put the roti away. I'll show you." Neela stuffed the remaining piece into her mouth. "Lie on your side," Renu said, turning onto her back and slipping her arm under Neela's while guiding her toward her shoulder until Neela's head came to rest against her neck. "Like this," she said.

Neela closed her eyes. The warmth of Renu's neck, the scent of her body, left Neela aching. Hollow. It was a feeling she could not describe. Though she *could* describe what it was not: it was not lonely, it was not sad. It was keenly felt but it caused no pain. It was not the skin of a banana. Nor the leaves of the dusty banyan tree. It was not hunger, not anymore.

On Neela's ninth day at the camp Babu came to fetch her. She was ushered into the tent by one of the camp administrators. "Your husband is here," the woman announced.

"That's impossible," Neela said. "He's dead."

The woman nodded toward the far end of the tent. And there he was, exactly as Neela remembered him: dry and depleted as if he'd been left out in the sun too long. She blinked and blinked and then she felt faint. It couldn't be. All the blood drained from her body. She heard a distant bell. She realized it was coming from within the camp, announcing lunch. She thought of all those women dressed in white saris, bald, smiling, filing into the mess tent. She was not among them. Her mouth filled with the bitterness of the liquid in the dark brown bottle. "But I thought—"

"I was never on that train," he said. "A whole week in a cell without a window. Stripping a man just to see if he's a Muslim. Lying, telling me my mother is dead. Those bastards, they're no better than animals."

He reached for her absently, as if reaching for fruit on a high branch. For fruit he barely wanted to eat. It occurred to her in that moment that her husband had not died. He had not. And that her life had taken yet another turn: she was no longer a widow. Neela also knew that from then on she would remain a fruit her husband didn't really want to reach, that he would watch ripen and fall with only a vague and stolid interest. She heard the laughter of the women in the camp. The sound came to her as if through a long and airy tunnel. She listened for Renu's. What reached her instead was Babu's voice saying, "Get your things. The bus leaves in ten minutes."

This time the bus ride seemed much longer than four hours. Neela was crushed against the window on the women's side of the bus. A fat mother with both children perched on her lap sat next to her. The older of the two children—a boy who Neela guessed was two or three—kicked and dug sharply into Neela's thighs. When Neela asked the woman to watch her boy's legs, she turned and glared at Neela and said, "Watch yours." Neela strained her neck trying to spot Babu, but he was too far back, on the men's side.

Near Rangarh the woman and her children disembarked and an old woman with gray-blue hair sat next to Neela. She held a small bundle in her lap close against her chest. Even on the dusty and crowded bus Neela could smell the clean, scrubbed scent of the old woman's skin, with only the slightest hint of sweat, almost pleasant, in the din of the bus.

Neela turned and looked out into the endless landscape of dirty fields and sparse, drooping trees. She closed her eyes. When she opened them the sun was setting; she must've dozed off. She noticed the old woman with the gray-blue hair leaning toward the man in the seat across from theirs, in the opposite aisle. He too was old. Neela pretended to be adjusting the bag at her feet to hear what they were saying. "They were plump, for the season," the man was saying.

"We should've bought more," the woman said, "I could've sent pickle to the girls."

The old man leaned closer. Neela realized they were husband and wife. "Rajan's coming by next week for the receipts. I'll tell him to bring another bushel."

"I thought he got them last week."

The bus bounced over a pothole. The old woman hugged the bundle closer.

"Did you take your medicine?"

"No, not yet," the old woman replied.

Neela turned toward the window. The landscape was the same though the wind had changed direction. She thought again of turning, looking for Babu, smiling, but she didn't. She only screened her eyes, shielding them from the dust.

The hut was just as she'd left it. Babu's pants still hung from the nail by the door. The reed mats were still folded neatly in the kitchen. The bag of rice stood untouched. Even the banyan tree looked as if not a wisp of wind had troubled it in the nine days Neela had been gone.

For dinner that night she made rice and dal and subzi with the eggplant Babu had purchased at the market on their way home from the bus stop. After they'd eaten she made two cups of tea and took them out to the banyan tree. Babu was sitting cross-legged beneath it. Earlier she'd noticed his eyes glisten with tears when he'd discovered that the police hadn't lied: his mother was dead. He'd stood at the door, stolen one quick glance at Neela then left the hut without a word. Now he was bent over something she could not see. When she handed him his tea she saw that it was her mangal sutra. She sat down beside him.

Babu took a sip of his tea. "I'm glad I found you," he said.

Neela turned to look at him. *He was?* A sudden warmth flooded her. Her fingers gripped the cup tighter as her thoughts tumbled and tripped over each other. She'd been wrong. He cared for her after all. He'd been lonely too. He just hadn't known how to show it but now he would. Now they'd show each other.

"That's the only way Lalla would give the mangal sutra back," he continued. "He said, 'Why do you need it? She's gone.' You should've seen the look on his face when I told him I'd found you." He finished his tea and held the empty cup out to Neela. "Hope that hair doesn't take long to grow back," he said. "Your head looks like a melon."

That night Babu took her, as Neela knew he would. Then he turned over and went to sleep. She lay awake for a long while afterward. The night was quiet, interrupted occasionally by the chirping of crickets, the wail of a dog. They'd moved their reed mat outdoors because of the heat. The branches of the banyan tree swayed in the hot wind and Neela lay in the dark, looking into them. How long had it stood there? Maybe hundreds of years. She thought of her mother and wondered whether she'd been cradled in her arms for even a moment before she'd died. She thought of her father. She even thought of the old lady on the bus with the gray-blue hair and the scent of her scrubbed skin. Then she thought of Renu. The plans they'd made, the cot they'd shared. She felt her eyes warm with tears. With hardly a thought, almost as if the decision had been waiting there all along, Neela rose soundlessly and walked back into the hut. She dug her fingers through the bag of rice and lifted the dark brown bottle out of the kernels.

And so there *was* one thing that was different: the color of the bottle no longer reminded her of the color of chocolate. Now it was simply a bottle, the thing it had always been.

She went back to the reed mat and lay down next to Babu. He was snoring lightly. She looked again into the branches. They fluttered and hummed with her every breath. The stars beyond spun like wheels. The branches reached down and just as she closed her eyes they gathered her up onto their shoulders and held her as she had always dreamed of being held. As she would never be held again.

THE MERCHANT'S MISTRESS

The first time Renu traveled as a man was while on her way to Ahmedabad. It happened like this: she had changed trains in Phulera, and was forced to buy a second-class ticket to Ahmedabad, in the women's compartment, because the third class was full. She seated herself in the corner of the berth, next to the window, and watched as the other passengers loaded their suitcases and bags bursting with food and thick winter blankets for the overnight journey. Renu had nothing to put away. She wore everything she owned in the world, including both her sweater and her shawl. Her remaining money, eight anna in all, was tucked into her pocket, and she had no need of toiletries: her hair was hardly an inch long, and whenever she passed a pump, she rinsed out her mouth and washed her hands and feet.

Across from her settled two young women. They looked about Renu's age, but they were clearly educated. One was reading a book and the other was looking over her friend's shoulder and then out of the window and then at Renu. Renu looked away. Beside her sat two little girls, one about five and the other eight or nine. Their father, a middle-aged man with thinning hair and a fat, boyish face, adjusted and readjusted their luggage. He looked sadly at the little girls, as if from sheer longing he could turn them into boys, and said, "Don't put your hands out of the window, do you hear? And listen to your mother."

They both nodded.

At this, the mother entered the berth. She was a wide woman, her breasts pendulous, even while obscured beneath her knit shawl, and her hair hennaed and pulled tight into a braid, a few strands aglow like copper in the fading light, framing her round face. Her eyes passed over her family and paused only when they reached the two young women. She seemed to approve. Then they stopped at Renu.

"You," she said. "What are you doing here? Do you see that, ji, there's a man in our berth."

It took a moment for Renu to realize she was talking about her. That she had mistaken her for a man. She opened her mouth to speak, but the woman continued, "Nakaam, creep, get out, or I'll call the police." She turned to her husband, who was staring at his wife. The young women were staring at Renu. "Ji," she told her husband. "Go call the conductor." She plopped down next to Renu, crossed her arms, and rested them on her round stomach.

The husband left the berth. Renu could no longer see the woman's daughters; her body blocked them completely. Only her face, now so close she could see the thin eyelashes, the plucked chin, the voluminous chest heaving with effort. She might've been beautiful once, Renu thought, before she had her daughters, before the husband's disappointments had colored her own, before life had been cruel, nearly meticulous, in its onslaughts, but now she was simply a fat, well-fed woman. It would never occur to her—once she'd decided on the matter—that Renu could be anything but a man.

Renu was intrigued. It made her feel somehow lighter. Then it gave her an idea.

She walked through to the men's compartment and settled into a slim space, in a seat facing the lavatory. All the men around her were smoking and playing cards and eating roasted peanuts and paid her no attention. She watched them for a while, careful not to bring attention to herself, and then fell into a deep and dreamless sleep.

Renu was nineteen when she left the refugee camp and traveled to Ahmedabad. It was the winter of 1949. She'd been there two years, just long enough to understand that she, along with the eight hundred other widows stationed at the camp, had absolutely no future ahead of them. Certainly, the government of India had been a passable guardian: they'd been fed, most days, and if they chose, the residents could enroll in vocational training programs to teach them various skills, such as how to be a seamstress. A darajin. Even the sound of the word was a dead end. Some of the younger and more beautiful widows, Renu noticed, had been pitied by a guard or a camp administrator and were married to them. Could pity combined with lust make a marriage? Renu didn't know, but what she did know was that she had no desire—none whatsoever, not even in the face of a bleak and empty future—to be a darajin.

The other thing Renu refused to do was let her hair grow out. All of the other widows at the camp were delighted when their bald heads began to sprout. The slightest fuzz and they'd scramble to affix an artless ribbon to the top of their heads, or vie for the one cracked mirror in the camp, admiring their woolly scalps, as if the hair were falling halfway down their backs. But Renu was mortified. What she loved—beyond even her own understanding—was the feel of the wind on her scalp. It reminded her of standing with her husband, Gopichand, who'd been killed by a Muslim mob two years ago, on their three scrubby acres of land, and gazing toward the blue and distant Shivalik Hills. She'd gazed like that, with his arms around her, and imagined that they would remain that way forever. Not literally, of course, but that the Shivaliks would stand like they always stood against the morning sky, whipped and creamy like clotted ghee, and that the dandelions would bend like baby's heads in the northeasterly wind, and that she would be a farmer's wife, with its days of toil and earth and anguish, measuring the rains as one measures sugar into a teacup, with care and constancy, and by the spoonful. And she assumed something further: that her destiny was like the small stream that ran at the edge of their property. That it would flow—diverted at times by a fallen branch or a pile of rock, true, and thinned in the dryness of summer while abundant in spring, undoubtedly—but

THE MERCHANT'S MISTRESS | 21

that essentially and always, it would flow, and be tied, deeply and incontrovertibly, to the destiny of the man to whom she clung.

Renu couldn't have been more wrong.

She understood this, in a terrible, twisted way, on the evening she watched the mob torch their hut, slaughter their goats, and decimate their three meager acres of wheat. She had run and jumped into the stream, hidden as it was by a slight ravine, and watched as the figures of the men danced in the flames. Then she looked to her left and her right. Her husband wasn't there. She thought he was behind her and maybe he had been, but he wasn't any longer. Renu arched her neck, but she still couldn't see him. So she crawled on her stomach to the top of the ravine. Her mouth filled with dust, her arms pushed against the crumbling dirt, her eyes lifted over the crest, and *that* was when she saw him. In the firelight. His head tilted back, the gleam of a knife against his throat, then a gesture that was unmistakable. And in that moment Renu understood one last thing: that nothing she'd imagined of her life, of her destiny, would ever come to pass. Not one thing remained. Not one, except—and these she saw as angry open mouths gnawing at the tender twilit sky—the Shivaliks still stood.

When she left the camp she was given twenty rupees and a pair of chappals. She tucked the money into an inside pocket of her shalwar—which she'd asked one of the darajins to sew for that express purpose—and then she put the chappals on her bare feet. It was almost as if the Indian government, in providing these last gifts, was saying, If money and a long walk won't get you there, nothing will. Renu stood at the entrance gate to the camp, wrapped in a wool shawl over her thick sweater, a man's—passed down to her after a resident who'd saved it as a memento of her late husband had herself died—and turned toward Mrs. Kaur, the camp director. She was staring at Renu's head.

"Where will you go?" she asked.

Renu shrugged. "I don't know. As far as the money will take me."

They stood silently. Renu thought of the life of the camp. Of all the women she'd never see again. She thought especially of Neela.

"You could've married again, you know," Mrs. Kaur said. "You were one of the prettiest ones. If only you'd let it grow out."

Renu pulled the shawl over her head. "But then I wouldn't have gotten the twenty rupees and the chappals, Mrs. Kaur."

"You're insolent. That's your other problem. Besides, a husband's worth far more than that."

"Is he?" Renu smiled.

Mrs. Kaur shook her head and called a rickshaw that was passing by the camp.

When Renu arrived at the train station, a few miles away, it was midday, and the next train was leaving for Chandigarh in twenty minutes. The train after that wasn't until eight o'clock in the evening, so Chandigarh, though not very far from Amritsar, was where she decided to go. She bought a third-class ticket, in the women's compartment, and arrived in Chandigarh that evening. She slept in a corner of the train station, her shawl spread on the stone floor, then took the morning train to Delhi. In Delhi she counted her money; she had fifteen rupees left. Now, from Delhi and with the fifteen rupees tucked into her shalwar, she had a number of choices: she could go to Bhopal, via Jhansi, she could travel to Mathura and then on to Varanasi, or she could go west, through Phulera and ending in Ahmedabad. Renu stood under the timetable of train departures. She breathed, hugging the sweater and shawl close against her body. South, east, or west?

She hailed a passing puri wallah and bought a packet of three puris with potato curry. She took the packet, stepping gingerly over the mass of sleeping bodies on the railway platform, through the main concourse and then outside, into the cold morning air. The sky was the color of kheer. A horde of rickshaws, bicycles, a few cars, and even an old horse-drawn brougham idled in the roundabout that fronted the railway station. A few men stood in groups, drinking chai and smoking beedies. She heard the wail of an approaching train and once it had subsided there descended from the Gothic arches and down the bloodred pillars of the station's facade a sudden silence. It was disturbing, lovely, and perfectly befit the first morning in two years that she had not woken to the harsh clang and peal of the bell at the camp. It was invariably followed by the rush of eight hundred women and children to the toilets, a fight for a cup of water from the three drums set next to the supply tent, and then came exactly what had come for the past two years: a long, listless day of waiting. For what? Renu never quite grasped for what. Food, certainly, that meager daily helping of roti and curry, but something else too. Something whose lack she'd felt but could never name. Neela, if she'd asked her, would've wrapped her arms around Renu in the dark, played her fingers against the hollow of Renu's neck, and whispered, "They're waiting for a guard to marry them, or for some lost family member to come and find them, they're waiting for their hair to grow out. But *we*, we aren't waiting for anything." And though it was true—Renu had been content, even after Neela had left—there was still a sense that there was something, *something* that was missing.

She threw her empty packet of puris into the gutter. A slight breeze blew in the scent of cardamom and woodsmoke, the pods of a semal tree were strewn on the ground, and next to the brougham was a coal brazier where an old man sat on his haunches, brewing coffee. She looked at him, and then she looked at the horse that was tied to the brougham. It was a dark velvety brown, rich as the coffee the old man was pouring into terra-cotta mugs, and though she and Gopichand had never owned a horse, she could sense in its presence something of their three acres: the swaying wheat, the undulant hills, the light of a small and welcoming fire. Just then the horse raised its head, from where it had been nibbling along the ground, and, gazing between its blinders, looked straight at Renu. They both blinked. Then the horse went back to its nibbling but Renu continued watching it. Its regal head, the tuft of hair between its ears, its wet nostrils, the blinders on the sides of each of its eyes. She wiped her hands against her shawl and wondered about the blinders. Why did they even put such things on a horse? No other animals were made to wear them, not that she could think of. So why a horse?

The driver of the brougham—chewing betel nut, a curling mustache bouncing above his blue uniform kurta as he did so—came out of the station and raised himself onto the seat. He pulled on the reins and the horse came to attention. Then he flicked them and the horse started up, clopping past Renu as it rounded away toward the exit. And then she saw it: the blinders were to focus the horse so it wouldn't be distracted, to keep it from looking sideways, to give it a straight course, a goal, to give the horse—and at this Renu smiled—purpose. And *that*, she realized, was what she'd been missing at the camp, what she'd been waiting for all along: purpose. Because once you had purpose, Renu understood, standing in the dim winter's morning light outside the Delhi train station, you had everything. You were a river knifing your way through a gorge of sheer rock and red cliff; everything you needed was inside of you. And not hunger, not fatigue, not the lack of money or means or even success, could sway the truly purposed. That too she understood.

By now the horse had nearly reached the end of the

esplanade leading away from the train station. Renu watched it go. When it reached the main road, she wondered, would it continue south, or would it turn and go east, or would it go west? The horse paused, and she saw the driver's arm reach out to adjust the reins, swat them against the horse's back, and then she saw it make its turn. West. Renu walked back under the Gothic arches of the train station and proceeded to the ticket counters.

She reached Ahmedabad the next morning. She wanted a bath so she walked from the railway station to the Sabarmati and, concealing her sweater and shawl under a thicket, waded into the river. The water was cold, silken, and when she dipped her head under it, it passed over her scalp with the thickness and the strength of a hand. Renu reemerged and saw a group of laundresses on the banks, beating piles of damp saris against the rocks. She waved to them but they only stared at her. She dripped a trail of water behind her as she approached them, her shalwar kameez soaked and clinging to her body. One of the laundresses, a young girl, bright with sunlight gleaming on her wet face, pointed at Renu's chest and laughed. "So you're a girl."

Renu laughed too, and asked them if she could help them in exchange for food. They laughed again, and said, "These saris are heavier than you are," and gave her a tin of chapati and rajma and curd. She ate every last morsel in the tin without stopping, licked it clean, and said, "Not anymore."

The girl who'd first spoken to her walked over to Renu and sat down next to her. She smelled of the freshness of soap, river silt, and sweat. Her skin was as dark as the horse's had been. "What else can you do?" she asked.

"Anything," Renu said. "Cook, clean, raise goats."

The young laundress giggled. "Did you hear that, Sindhu, goats!" One of the other girls looked over and shook her head. Renu and the young laundress turned back to the river. It was swifter now; the wind had picked up, and from the west rushed a bank of gray clouds. "I've heard the memsahib needs a new maid. When can you start?" the laundress asked.

"Now," Renu said.

The memsahib was the beautiful, young wife of a diamond merchant. That evening, when Renu met her, she was sitting on her divan with so many glittering jewels covering her neck and face that she drowned out the light of the oil lamps that surrounded her. Renu stared at her with open curiosity and awe.

The memsahib smiled luxuriously and said, "You've never seen this many jewels, have you?"

"I've never seen *a* jewel," Renu said.

"What do you think of them?"

"I think you'd be more beautiful without them."

There was silence. Renu looked at her and sensed the kind of sadness she had sensed in Neela. But why should a destitute girl in a refugee camp and the wealthy wife of a diamond merchant have the same kind of sadness? "Well," the mem-sahib said after a few moments, "are you just going to stand there or are you going to fetch me my slippers?"

That was the only indication Renu was to ever get that she was hired. She worked steadily and satisfactorily for the memsahib. In the mornings, her duties were to bring the memsahib's breakfast, massage her hair with oils, draw her bath, and then help her to dress. In the afternoons all her maids gathered and they either played games or one sang and played the flute while the memsahib, whose name was Savitri, napped or practiced her sitar. The evenings were busiest, and always tense. Renu rushed to draw the memsa-hib another bath, and helped her to prepare for the mer-chant's attentions: her hair was plaited with flowers, jewelry was selected with great care, scents and oils were applied. Only once, after her bath, did the memsahib sigh and whis-per, "What does it even matter?"

Renu paused in stringing a garland of flowers. "How do you mean, memsahib?" she asked.

"He's always in an opium haze, anyway."

And so *there* was the reason for the sadness, Renu real-ized. And maybe it was because of this sadness, or maybe because of the way Renu looked at her—without lowering her eyes like the other maids—that she, within a month of arriving in Ahmedabad, became the memsahib's lover.

This went on for two years. The memsahib would go to her husband's bedroom and when she returned late into the night, she stripped off her jewels and left a trail of them leading from the door to the bed, where Renu waited for her. And it was true, what she had said: the memsahib was far more beautiful without her jewels. Sometimes, before she had even finished undressing, Renu would pull her into the bed and kiss her deeply, she would take the chunni that drifted from her shoulders and tie up her hands. Then she would tickle the loose ends of the chunni over her body until Savitri squealed with delight before wrapping it tightly around her slender neck. It was only then that Renu lowered herself between her legs. Savitri would gasp for breath, but then she would also smile. Renu once loosened the chunni and asked, "What if your husband finds out?"

Savitri lolled her head to the side and sighed and said, "Then you'll be led to the Sabarmati, if you're lucky."

Renu retightened the cloth and a tingle went down her spine. She wondered at it—at the coldness of the memsahib's words—and knew the end was inevitable. That the end would come. And if it were to catch her unawares then no one— not the memsahib, not her wits, nothing—would save her.

It was around this time, during the third year that Renu was in the diamond merchant's employ, that she actually spoke to him for the first time. She was walking past the veranda one evening, on her way to the memsahib's quarters, when she heard two men talking. One, the much older of the two, was hunched over a thick ledger while the other, whom she'd never seen before but was clearly the diamond merchant—

with his silk kurta embroidered in gold, polished hands, and air of gentility—was looking out toward the vast gardens that surrounded the house.

"It's always two, never more than two," the man with the ledger was saying.

The diamond merchant looked at the old man, seemed to consider the statement, and said, "Then it can't be him. It must be a counting mistake. He could steal any number if he wanted to. Why always two?"

Renu stopped on the marble steps leading up the veranda and said, "Two what?"

Both men turned to stare. The old man might've even gasped. Renu stood absolutely still. She held her breath. The words had simply come out of her, and she braced for whatever would come next. "The impudence!" the old man shouted, his lips quivering. "How dare you speak to the sahib." But the diamond merchant only looked at her curiously. "Diamonds," he said, smiling. "Two diamonds."

"He, whoever he is, will never steal more," Renu said, ascending a step, braver. "That's what he'll always steal: two."

"And how is it that you know that?" the merchant asked. The old man, by now, seemed in a state of shock. He was practically torpid.

"Because we had a woman in our camp, nice woman, with two small sons. She was in charge of making the morning roti. And every afternoon we would always come up eight short. Always eight. Not seven, not nine. Eight. When we asked her about it she said they were being stolen by a colony of monkeys that lived nearby, in the trees surrounding the camp. But that couldn't be true, could it? Monkeys don't count out eight. So we realized it had to be her, because that's how people are: they like order, they tend toward it. She was, of course, taking the same number every day to feed her sons. And this man, whoever is stealing the diamonds, only takes two. He always will."

Both men were silent for a moment. Then the diamond merchant laughed out loud. He turned to the old man. "Who is she?" he asked.

"One of the memsahib's maids," he replied.

The diamond merchant seemed to consider this for a moment then he leaned over and whispered something in the old man's ears. The old man's expression soured, but he nodded. And that is how Renu came to be summoned to the diamond merchant's quarters the following afternoon.

The diamond merchant's quarters were even more opulent than the memsahib's. Renu was led into the main room through a series of long stone and marble hallways; there were exquisite temple sculptures along the walls, and lush carpets on the floors. She heard the tinkle of water as they neared the main room and realized, when she entered it, that it was coming from a pink marble fountain in the center of the room. Four maidens rose out of the water, offering lotuses and with eyes that Renu could only assume were rubies. Beyond was a bed covered in sheets of shimmering silk and gold and beyond even that was a row of sculpted pillars that led into a private garden that Renu had never seen. And there, leaning against one of the pillars and looking out over the garden, stood the diamond merchant.

The servant who had shown her here had left, Renu noticed with dismay. She raised her chunni over her bald head and wondered whether to address the diamond merchant or wait for him to address her. She waited. After some minutes passed—during which Renu studied the women in the fountain—the merchant, without once turning around, said, "How long do you plan on standing there?"

Renu picked up her lehenga and hurried toward him. She stopped just before she reached him. He turned to face her. His face was still smooth, but his hair was thinning, she noticed. He had the same air of richness, of wealth, as the memsahib, but unlike her, whose expression was alert and sometimes anxious, he seemed bored. Bored in a way that Renu couldn't possibly understand, not while standing in the most beautiful room she'd ever seen, not with a private garden, and a fountain, and a bed so richly made.

He brushed her chunni from her head and smiled sadly and said, "You look like the boy I always wanted to be."

Then he looked at her, for so long that Renu didn't think it possible without blinking. She wondered if that was her cue to do something but she couldn't imagine what that might be. She raised her eyes to his and saw that he was hardly there; that his eyes had such a faraway look in them, a look of such forlornness that she wondered if it was best to simply leave. But then he took her hand. He gripped it, really, and it seemed to Renu that now he was pleading with her. Not pleading, no, but searching. Searching for something he had lost. As if she might know where it was. As if she might help him find it. Renu started to say she hadn't the slightest clue, how could she, without even knowing what it was, but as soon as she opened her mouth he covered it with his, and kissed her.

And so that was how Renu came to be a lover to both the diamond merchant and the diamond merchant's wife. Her days were divided between them. In the late afternoons she visited the merchant. They made love, then she filled his opium pipe and talked to him while he smoked—about her life, about the camp, once even about Neela—until he fell into a deep fog. Then he would wave her away. The evenings were the same as they had been: she helped the memsahib prepare for her evening with the diamond merchant, and then waited for her in her bed. The arrangement, if either was aware of it, didn't seem to bother them. Besides, as Renu soon came to realize, the wealthy had only one rule: anything was allowed, or at least considered, as long as it didn't diminish their wealth.

During one of her afternoons with the diamond merchant, after he'd begun to smoke, he asked her to tell him a story.

"What kind of story?" Renu asked.

"One that you heard a long time ago," he said.

"A long time ago?"

She thought for a moment and then she began. "Once upon a time," she said, "there lived a king with three sons. Now this king was old, and he knew he was going to die soon, but he wanted to leave his kingdom to his most worthy son. The one who would preserve it, be frugal with it. And so he decided to test them. He gave each of his sons a hundred rupees and an empty room. He told them that whoever could fill the room—fill it completely, without a single empty pocket of space—for the least amount of money would inherit his kingdom.

"He returned the following week and went to the eldest son's room. The eldest son gave him eighty rupees back and the king saw that he'd filled the room with discarded paper. Old newspapers, really. And that he'd stuffed them into every corner of the room. The king nodded approvingly and went to the second son's room. This son gave him ninety rupees back. The king was pleased, and saw that he'd filled the room with garbage. Lots and lots of garbage. But it was ingenious, and he'd only spent ten rupees. So then the king went to his youngest son's room. Now when he reached this room, his son gave him ninety-nine rupees back. The king, as you can imagine, was astonished. 'But how,' he cried, 'how could you possibly fill a room with one rupee?'

"The youngest son smiled. He opened the door and in the middle of it was a lit candle. The room was filled with light. 'I spent seventy-five paisa on the candle,' the son said, 'and twenty-five paisa for a box of matches.' The king was overjoyed, and so the youngest son, to great fanfare, was crowned king."

At the end of the story Renu looked over at the diamond merchant, but he was asleep. Or at least his eyes were closed. Renu studied his face, in the dim of late afternoon, with the sweetness of the opium smoke drifting around her. All trace of boredom and pleading and searching were gone, his face was as simple and as incorruptible as a child's. She wondered if that was an effect of the opium, or if that was his true self. Beyond that she wondered at how fond she'd grown of him. She wondered that she might even be in love with him.

The end came. The end did come. It was during one of Renu's afternoons with the diamond merchant. She was packing his pipe, and he was watching her. "I'm sailing for Durban next week," he said casually. "I'll be back in three months."

Renu looked up. "Durban? Where is that?"

"It's in South Africa."

"Where's that?"

The diamond merchant rose from his divan and went to a teakwood cabinet in the corner of the room. He took a key from the inside of his silk kurta and opened it. Inside Renu saw a stack of bills, and boxes, and sheets rolled and tied with ribbon. It was one of these that the diamond merchant extracted and placed before Renu. She looked at him and then she untied it. It was a map, and though Renu had never seen one, she understood what it was immediately. It took her breath away. It was the most beautiful thing she had ever seen: the thick creamy paper, the countries strung together like jewels, the sprawling blue of all the seas she'd never seen.

"Where is it?" she asked again.

He pointed to Durban.

"And where are we?"

He pointed to Ahmedabad. Renu gasped. "So far away," she said, breathing.

That night she lay in bed and thought about the map. Not so much about the map as what it meant. And she thought about the events of her life, none of them very interesting, she had to admit, but each of them a stepping-stone across a strange and lonely place. The diamond merchant would leave, and then he would return. Their triangle would continue, and then they would all grow old, old, old. In the end the diamond merchant and Savitri would have their money, and each other, but what would Renu have?

The thought of what she must do made her sad but Renu knew that every moment from when she'd stood outside the Delhi train station—every single one—had led to this one.

On the afternoon before the diamond merchant was due to depart, Renu came to him as usual. She wore her most beautiful lehenga, a deep turquoise with silver threading. When she entered he took her to his bed without a word and made love to her. Afterward she smiled at him, she took his face in her hands and placed it over her bare chest. He said, sleepily, "You know what, Renu? You're the candle and the match." Renu let out a cry. His words, his hot breath against her breasts seemed to her the truest effluence of love, and she thought for a moment—the briefest moment—that she would not do as she had planned.

In the end she sat beside him while he lay on his divan, and packed his opium pipe. He was talking about the mines he was to visit in South Africa. He had been there many times, and he told her about the people there, how dark and different they looked, how mysterious and bold and so black they were almost purple. He told her about the endless plains, reaching to a distant and knifelike horizon. He paid her no attention. And Renu, listening attentively, continued to pack his pipe. It was more than was necessary, but she could take no chances.

She waited while he smoked it. She leaned against his divan and watched. He closed his eyes. She continued to wait. She waited until the moon came up over his garden. The silver light creeping like hands across the grass and over the marble floor. She decided, Until it reaches my feet, that's how long I'll wait. And so she waited. And only when the moonlight touched the very tip of her heel did she rise and press her head against the diamond merchant's chest, making certain it was still.

She took the key from under his kurta, opened the teak cabinet, and took out the stack of bills. But she had to open all the boxes to find what she was actually looking for. When she did she emptied the contents of the pouch onto her palm. And even in the moonlight they glistened, and they reminded her of the Shivaliks, their summits so pure, covered in snow and crystalline and shining, treacherous, and as deadly as diamonds.

The ship's manifest recorded the diamond merchant as having boarded. Renu was shown, by no other than the ship's captain, to her cabin. She had practiced deepening her voice so that when the captain said, "Does it suit your needs, sir?" Renu paused, settled the air deep in her throat, and said, "It'll do."

And it would: it was three large rooms, furnished handsomely, and she was provided with a personal servant. She waited for the captain to leave, and then she readjusted the pouch in the inside of her kurta, straightened her cap in the mirror, and realized the hardest part was over. She breathed, she let out a smile; she sat on the bed and thought not about the country she was leaving but about the people she'd already left. She thought about Gopichand, and the naïve, young love she had felt for him. She thought about Neela, sweet, scarred Neela, and how their love had defied everything—the hunger in the camp, the loneliness, the deprivation—until her husband had reappeared one day and taken her away. And she thought about the diamond merchant, the one who—in her own way—she had loved the most. She wondered first how long it would take them to notice the newly turned earth on the edge of his private garden. Then she wondered if she would ever love another as much as she had the diamond merchant, but it didn't seem possible. It didn't seem possible that the heart could hold so much love, that it could hold so much and still keep itself from breaking.

One morning, at the end of the third week on the ship, the lookout sighted land. He yelled down from the crow's nest and all the passengers scampered onto the deck to have a look. Renu saw it from the starboard side. At first it was only a thin line at the edge of the horizon. And for hours that's all it was: a thin line. But even after all the other passengers had drifted away Renu remained on deck. She watched that thin line until evening then she went to sleep and woke up and watched it again. By now the coastline of Africa was clearly visible. She saw a cluster of outcroppings that looked like rocks; she realized they were buildings. The water became even bluer. It turned the turquoise of the lehenga she had left behind when she'd stolen the diamond merchant's clothes. And then the wind shifted. It turned warm. And Durban came into view. She looked at it with pleasure, with such delight that her heart seemed to swell. And the warmth of the wind carried with it the scent of Africa. The scent of its soft green endlessness, its cracked roads and flat-topped trees, its red and lonely cliffs that baked under the hot sun. It smelled of its teeming cities and dusty bush, its antique shores pounded by so many seas, its breathless summer nights. She felt like she had been lifted from a previous life and placed here, on this ship, on the cusp of this vast and unknowable continent, the interior beckoning her like a moonlit road. But those roads would all come later. For now Renu let the warmth sweep through her and for the fourth and final time, she fell in love.

THE IMPERIAL POLICE

Jenkins drank his morning tea and waited. It'd been three days since Abheet Singh's death. His wife had already been informed, but it was required that the head constable make an official report to the family of the deceased. Jenkins took a sip of his tea. He looked out into the main room of the police station. It was empty; the subinspectors were out questioning the villagers. A pall of heat hung over the room, the walls dripped morosely. The fan too seemed wilted in the heat, ticking off the mournful seconds like a metronome. He watched it with interest, wondering what she would be like. He guessed she would most likely be silent, weeping, a bit unattractive; these village women aged prematurely from working in the fields all day. He hardly knew what to say to her, his own eyes warmed with tears at the thought of Abheet Singh; he looked down at his wrist instinctively.

But it was peculiar: in the short time that Jenkins had held the post of head constable, with Abheet Singh as his subordinate, he'd not so much as mentioned his wife. Nor children, if he'd had any. That omission had filled Jenkins with a vague and guilty hope. He'd reasoned, while Abheet Singh was still alive, that these Indian—and soon to be Pakistani—villagers arranged all their marriages in childhood. How absurd. Who knew how one would turn out? Maybe, he'd concluded tentatively, Abheet Singh was just like him. The mere thought had made the heat rise to Jenkins's face yet here he was: waiting for his widow. How could he even look at her? There'd be hardly any need, he decided, these village women barely raised their heads, hidden as they were beneath all those veils and burqas and some such nonsense. Still, he wondered.

The morning of Abheet Singh's death, only three days ago, was exceptionally hot. Jenkins had taken a rickshaw in, though he generally preferred to walk, but he'd slept badly the night before. It'd been four weeks since he'd arrived in Rawalpindi but he still couldn't abide the heat, or the thoughts of Abheet Singh. And so finding Abheet Singh waiting, hands clasped behind his muscular back, nearly sent Jenkins tumbling over a chair as he strode toward his desk. He recovered, stripped off his coat, the heat already prickling his skin, and grew curiously and painfully agitated. He pushed away the feeling and took a deep breath. Meanwhile, Abheet Singh saluted his lamely executed salute, and stood waiting next to the doorway.

"What is it?" Jenkins said, looking down, shuffling through some papers and feigning annoyance.

"A couple of the stalls were burned down early this morning, sir. In the main bazaar."

Jenkins sighed. So it had reached Rawalpindi. "Muslim or Hindu?"

"Sikh."

Jenkins might've guessed. Once he gathered the courage to take a long look at Abheet Singh—lifting his gaze from the desk to his face, lingering on the turn of his jaw, angled and strong even with the beard covering it and leading rapturously into that turban, the silken sheaths of hidden hair driving him to distraction, forcing him to focus—even Jenkins could see that Abheet Singh's eyes were anguished, glistening; his own people had been attacked.

"Bring the jeep," he ordered after a moment but then regretted it immediately. A kind word first might've been more appropriate. Abheet Singh seemed not to notice. He only saluted again, turned, and this time Jenkins noticed that his hand didn't even attempt to reach his brow but collapsed just short of his reddening eyes.

Still, the salute hadn't been the first thing Jenkins had noticed about Abheet Singh. The first thing he'd noticed, upon his arrival in Rawalpindi, was Abheet Singh's meticulousness. His shoes were always spotless, his uniform and turban, even in the blistering Rawalpindi heat, perfectly pressed. He was always the first to arrive at the police station, located just south of the main marketplace. And he completed every task he was assigned with such alacrity that it seemed nearly out of place in this small, remote desert town. Jenkins had requested this post six months ago. He'd been party to a small scandal back in Delhi—nothing he chose to dwell on, though the fact that it'd been based entirely on rumor had left in him a feeling of profound and inexplicable tiredness—and the isolation of this northwest frontier town suited him perfectly.

He'd arrived in April, when all his former colleagues at Delhi Cantonment had been making preparations to spend the hottest summer months in the mountains, Shimla or Haridwar probably. Most of them had not even bothered to say good-bye, nodding imperceptibly as they passed his desk on his last day, their eyes averted with embarrassment. Or maybe pity. He could see them now: sitting on their vast verandas, under the cool shade of the Himalayas, sipping their Pimm's and watching the bruised and tender green of the foothills with the same malevolent attention with which they'd watched him.

The police station in Rawalpindi was composed of three rooms. The main room was the public area with a stone floor, a long counter, two thin wooden benches by the entrance— along which the town drunks, the only ones the police ever had occasion to pick up in this small town, tottered and tipped over—and an overhead fan that knocked and swung and brayed like the devil. Every day Jenkins was sure it would come unfastened and fly out of the window. The fan had the pull of the devil too; he watched it with such contempt and such longing during the sweltering hours of the afternoon that it sometimes felt to him like love. He had a direct view of it from his open door; beyond it was the third room of the police station, which was just a straw-filled holding cell. Sometimes, if they were repeats or if their wives threatened to beat them, Jenkins let the drunks sleep it off in the cell. But usually it was empty, and it was in front of this darkened cell that Jenkins had first espied Abheet Singh's affliction.

Was it an affliction? It was a mystery, no doubt, because despite his impeccable and almost fastidious devotion to his appearance, Abheet Singh was glaringly casual in one regard: his salutation. He of course saluted Jenkins, as his superior officer, promptly every morning and evening, but the way he raised his hand to his forehead had none of the fervor and precision of his other duties. In fact it was downright sloppy.

It was because of this strange gesture that Jenkins began studying him during his second week in Rawalpindi. He did this surreptitiously, only when they were in the public areas of the station, and only when Abheet Singh saluted the other officer under Jenkins, Subinspector Iqbal. His two subordinates could not have been more different. Iqbal was corpulent and overly garrulous, mildly and gratingly obsequious; Jenkins guessed that a wealthy uncle, and bribes, had gotten him the position of subinspector. Abheet Singh, on the other hand, was a slim reserved man, young, in his early twenties. From his file Jenkins knew he'd already been married five years, probably in his late teens like all Sikh boys from the rural villages. His face itself, unlike the faces of the other young men in the village—fawning at the first sight of Jenkins, only to fall vacant once he passed—was like the desert that surrounded Rawalpindi. Somber and alive. The light in his eyes heaved and fell like the windswept sands. Even his skin was the color of sand dunes. Jenkins—who'd not met a single Indian during all his time in England—could practically feel the heat of the entire subcontinent rising from the bodies of these lovely brown men.

Abheet Singh's was no exception.

Though what drove Jenkins to utter distraction was his salute. He eyed it with increasing irritation with each passing day: first Abheet Singh's right arm would rise, as expected, but then his wrist would twist at a bizarre angle, palm out instead of down, just as his hand neared his forehead. He'd hold it there for far longer than was needed, almost as if he were drawing attention to it. Then his arm would fall back to his side, uncontrolled, the limb plummeting as lifeless as a dead bird. And with that the whole gesture concluded lamely, hurriedly, and Abheet Singh would avert his eyes like a child caught misbehaving. The motion was slow, lazy, and lacked even an iota of the crispness of military movements.

The first few times Jenkins had watched him he'd decided it was simply a sign of indolence. But that made no sense; he'd never seen Abheet Singh move so much as a pen without ensuring that it was laid straight against the edge of the desk. He then decided it was some form of insubordination. He'd wake at night, unable once again to sleep from the heat, and wonder at Abheet Singh's gesture. Could it be mocking him? At Delhi Cantonment the other officers had complained constantly about the newly trained Indians. It was the tropical treachery inherent to the Indians and the kaffirs, they said, Sikhs and Muslims and Hindus alike. Look at how they're killing each other off and the native police not doing a thing about it, they'd said smugly in the months leading to Partition. "Wouldn't know proper regimental training and order if it bit them on the bum," Smithson had said. They'd been in the canteen on a winter afternoon, the light of the sun yellow and inflamed, when Hughes had given Jenkins a sidelong glance and said, "Some here might even be keen on biting them on the bum." The next day Jenkins had requested transfer, and reddened even now, as he lay in bed well away from Delhi, at the insult. Still, he hadn't believed them, not completely. It was true that the Indians were slow learners and a bit smelly but they weren't treacherous, Abheet Singh least of all. But there was something about him, so much, really. His beautiful skin, his strong, muscular forearms, and all that silken hair piled on the top of his head, hidden under his turban. His beard was trimmed but Jenkins knew that Sikh men—that husky, ancient race of warriors—were forbidden to cut their hair. How long was it? Did it fall in a great wash down his back when he undid his turban, or was it tied up in some way? How did it look, spread across his pillow? The questions kept coming and Jenkins grew even warmer from the rush of heat to his middle. He sat straight up in bed. Well. This was unacceptable; it simply had to stop. He came to a decision, right then in the middle of the night: he simply must talk to Abheet Singh. Such a gesture, such total lack of discipline was inexcusable. How could a country even *hope* to govern itself with such obvious lack of self-control?

The question of self-control—it *had* been a question of self-control, hadn't it—recalled to him the piano lessons his mother insisted that he take well into his adolescence. So that while all the other boys were out playing cricket and looking at pictures in laddie magazines, Jenkins was stuck at home practicing piano. He'd been miserable at first—especially since his best friend, Toddy, was captain of the cricket team. But then Mrs. Bunting had retired and his mother had hired the new director of the church choir, Mr. Templeton, to give him lessons on the side. Before the first lesson Mr. Templeton, who'd read classics at Oxford, had knocked on the door and when Jenkins had opened it the sight of him had nearly knocked him off his feet. He'd never laid eyes on a man so perfectly formed: gray eyes as gloomy as the sea, hands and neck wiry yet formidable, thick dark hair that needed a cut fell over his ears and tickled his neck. He stood so erect, so blissfully unaware of his own handsomeness that Jenkins actually blushed. After that Jenkins didn't once complain or miss his piano lessons. In fact it got so that he was downright promising at it.

Of course, then came the incident in the church vestiary, when he and Mr. Templeton were found in what the vicar had called "an unfortunate position." Within a week Mr. Templeton was transferred to a parish in Wales and Jenkins, as his mother wept and his father looked away shamefacedly, boarded a train for Warwick. When the train pulled out of the station Jenkins stuck his head out of the window. He wanted to wave but he couldn't. His mother was still crying, but now she'd laid her head against his father's shoulder, while his arm held her to him. They stood like that—leaning against each other—for as long as Jenkins watched them. And it was *that*, that simplicity of feeling that Jenkins knew he'd somehow lost.

Even Mr. Templeton, after being found in the vestiary, when they were waiting for the vicar in his office, had said, "Deny it. Deny everything."

"But *how*," Jenkins said. "He saw us."

Mr. Templeton leaned toward him. "Make him doubt what he saw."

"That'd be lying."

"No," he said. "It'd be concealing the truth."

Jenkins looked at him. It seemed hard to believe that this had been the same person who'd held him to his beating chest, who'd kissed him only moments ago. The vicar, in the end, made it clear he wanted only for them to be out of his parish. "The empire's vast," he said, showing them to the door. "Try, if you could, not to come back."

And so Jenkins had been sent off to boarding school. Though, even at the age of sixteen, it seemed absurd to Jenkins that he should be sent to a boarding school for *boys*. The two years he remained at Warwick—along with the two or three tousles he had while there—did nothing more than solidify his sense that he was different, and that what he did must always be kept concealed, and that for him, in spite of the ache that had settled into his chest, clogged the passageways to his heart, there was no greater peace than the peace of another's arms. And so what, he thought, bracing against the cold of the long West Midland winters, if the arms happened to be those of another boy?

There had, of course, been no need for Jenkins to summon Abheet Singh; he'd been waiting for him in his office early that Monday morning. Once he'd brought the jeep around they'd headed into the village. They didn't return to the station for another twelve hours.

The looting had spread. Stores in the mainly Sikh and Hindu populated city center were locked as of midday. Jenkins imposed a curfew from noon till the next morning. They'd patrolled the streets for hours, chasing after small itinerant fires and skirmishes, crumbs thrown along their path just to taunt them. Jenkins, with Abheet Singh driving, rounded corner after corner only to see the marauding gangs vanish into a narrow alley or a nondescript doorway. They'd race to the end of the street, or the alleyway, and find a silence so deep it was as if the gang had simply vanished into thin air, as if it'd never existed.

They'd reached one such alley when Jenkins jumped out of the jeep and yelled, "Where the devil did they go?"

"It's easy to outrun the English, sir," Abheet Singh said calmly. "You never go anywhere without your jeeps."

So they abandoned it under a peepal tree and set out on foot. By then the sky burned white with heat, the last of the sun's rage before it began its descent, and the sand blew straight into their eyes. After half an hour of this Jenkins knew it was of no use. They headed back toward the jeep. As they neared the peepal tree Abheet Singh was the first to notice. "Sir, the tires," he gasped. All four had been slashed. They ran to it as if they could staunch its wounds but the air had let out long ago and the jeep rested, sleepy and bemused, on its axles. They looked around them; the street and the market were deserted.

"At least the curfew's working, sir," Abheet Singh said.

"Yes, well," Jenkins said. "That's the only time things work in this country: when you don't want them to."

They left the jeep under the peepal tree and began walking. Jenkins looked back at the jeep ruefully, as if it might be following them like a stray dog.

By now the sun was beginning to set. The sky glowed with streaks of burnt orange and a pale and luminous green. Jenkins felt a thin breeze from the west though it was still hot. He wiped his face with a handkerchief; he was exhausted, the heat was dizzying. He felt strangely broken by it, and by the day, and by Delhi. He looked around him—at the endless desert sands and the houses made of earth and the thin dusty grasses wheezing in the wind and Abheet Singh walking beside him, his face alert and beautiful against the barren land—and it occurred to him that the vicar was right: he could never return to England. That just the thought of Warwick and the Midlands and his mother and his father and even the pubs and the cricket matches and the afternoon teas had become unbearable for him, that it was this barren land, in the end, that seemed to him the promised one.

Maybe it was because of this thought that Jenkins shuddered, or maybe it was the one that followed: that he would soon *have* to leave, Pakistan would be born in a month's time, and what need would they have for him, for any of the British? He thought of the days ahead, and the days upon days that awaited him, and all the concealment of these many long years and he thought in that moment that he could not take another step, that really, there were no steps left to be taken.

Abheet Singh stopped in midstride. "Sir," he said, "you're trembling."

Jenkins looked down at his hands. His baton shook like a divining rod over water. His palms were clammy, cold, and yet his body burned and shook with sorrow; he gripped one arm with the other. "It's nothing," he said quickly. "Feeling a bit off, is all."

Abheet Singh looked from his hands into his eyes. They were within sight of the police station, tucked behind a high gate. The road in front led off toward the marketplace in one direction and the emptiness of the desert in another. The country all around was quiet. But for the two of them it hardly seemed inhabited. Only the sparrows had ventured into the treetops, chirping as the sun set. Abheet Singh looked a long while into Jenkins's eyes then slowly, almost tenderly, he reached toward him, wrapped his hand around his trembling wrist, and stilled it. The motion was so delicate, so utterly benevolent and sexless, that Jenkins could hardly breathe, and in that moment he thought he might've come to know, for the briefest moment, the thing for which he'd always yearned, the thing that was the opposite of his many, many lonely years, the opposite—at this, he closed his eyes—of his concealment.

When he thought back over the incident he could never decide what had come first: had Abheet Singh released his wrist first or had Jenkins looked away first. Though what he did recall with great clarity was that afterward he'd rushed through the station gates, straight past Iqbal, and disappeared into his office. He'd closed the door—something he'd never before done—and splashed water on his face from the bowl on the washstand. The water was nearly as hot as his skin. He'd then thrown himself into his chair, rose, paced then slumped back into the chair. He could still feel Abheet Singh's hand on his wrist. The touch had seared, branded itself into his skin. In his recollections, even moments later as he sat at his desk, he felt their pulses pounding against each other's like the sea against rock. How terrifying and how beautiful. Jenkins took a deep breath. But he must focus, he had no time to waste: he had to write the day's report, submit it to the head office in the morning. He picked up his pen and was just beginning to write on his decision to impose the curfew when there was a knock on the door.

Jenkins held his voice steady. "Come in."

Subinspector Iqbal stepped in and smiled mischievously. Did he know about the touch? He saluted Jenkins, with the proper knifelike motion, and waited for him to speak.

"What is it, Subinspector?"

"More trouble, sir. More of the shops have been looted."

"Who is it this time?" Jenkins sighed.

"The Hindus, of course." Iqbal said this with lavish seriousness, but Jenkins thought he saw the faintest smile drift across his face. He grimaced; he couldn't withstand another scandal.

"Don't just stand there," Jenkins shouted. "Get Singh and get out there!" Just saying his name sent a shiver through him.

"But sir, the jeep."

"Forget the jeep. You can't catch them in a jeep."

Iqbal hung his head and scooted out miserably. Jenkins sent a telegram to the head office: LOOTING SPREADING. NEED VEHICLE, PERSONNEL. NO CASUALTIES. Then he too headed to the marketplace on foot. It took him twenty minutes to reach it, even half-jogging part of the way. He broke into a full sprint when the smell of fire reached him.

Still it was useless, and far worse than he'd imagined; the curfew had been pointless. The market was razed. The five or six shops around the main square had been torched. Most of the wares had been carried off but the shelves were dragged into the square and burned. Charred bits of wood stuck out of the earth like scarecrows. The stalls too lay collapsed in a heap, no better than rags. Aside from a mangy dog poking around the stalls—sniffing for the fragrant sweetmeats that had tumbled from their displays—the entire square was empty. Where the hell were Iqbal and Abheet Singh? Jenkins heard shouts in the distance, coming from the north side of the market. He rushed toward the clamor of voices, the roar of footsteps. He ran through the maze of streets, turned left at the peepal tree and there, at the end of an alley, was a crowd of villagers, ten deep, gathered around something Jenkins couldn't see.

"*Chal!*" he yelled, pushing through the crowd, "*Chal!*"

They only pressed closer. A hand reached for his baton, another—thick and vehement—gripped his arm. He shook free of it, grabbed his baton, and clubbed his way toward the center.

He saw Iqbal first, at the head of the mob, and then he saw Abheet Singh, on the ground. Blood had already begun seeping into the dirt. His turban had been ripped from his head and lay some distance away, unmoving, as if it too had been wounded. Abheet Singh's hair had come loose. Jenkins looked at it until his eyes blurred then he slid to the ground. He reached out his hand—it *was* the earth trembling, wasn't it—and stroked Abheet Singh's hair. It was silken, as he'd known it would be, and so dark that he could well imagine diving into its pool at midnight. He knelt lower, gathered fistfuls of it and lifted them to his face, his mouth, swallowing back tears. It was then, as he bent his head into Abheet Singh's hair, that the smell of sweat and rust and desert sage and all those bodies pressed together made him swoon. He could hardly rise, and only then with Iqbal's help.

The day after Abheet Singh's death Jenkins had filed a full report with the head office. They'd responded two days later by sending additional inspectors to assist in what they had termed a "shoddy and obtuse" investigation. While Jenkins waited for Abheet Singh's wife the new inspectors and Iqbal were in the field interrogating every villager and shop owner in Rawalpindi. The straw-filled holding cell was now crowded with suspects. The district superintendent, along with the inspectors, had sent a further brittle message to Jenkins: "The circumstances leading to Subinspector Abheet Singh's death are under review, as is your service with the Imperial Police."

He read the note again then threw it into the dustbin. He could already see the gray, grimy shores of England.

He took another sip of his tea; he waited. Yes, she'd be easy enough to deal with, he considered, if only she wouldn't ask too many questions. Well, that was hardly a concern; he'd never heard an Indian woman *speak*, let alone ask a question. It occurred to him that she might be pretty. That was disconcerting, yes, though improbable. But she *had* been touched by him, they both had, and there was a fineness to that: being touched by a beautiful man.

He heard footsteps. After a slight shuffling two figures, a young woman and an old man, appeared just outside his door. So she's brought someone with her, Jenkins sniffed, I might've guessed. He nodded for them to enter but the woman gestured to the old man to wait on the bench. It was only after he was seated that she stepped into Jenkins's office. She stood for a moment, slim, wearing a lavender shalwar with a thin white veil pulled over her shoulders and hair. Her skin was pale, shimmering in the yellow light that pushed through the window, and from what Jenkins could see of her downturned face she had a rounded chin and plain features, almost crude, so unlike the rarefied features of her husband.

"Please," Jenkins gestured, "please sit down."

She walked to the chair, her eyes still cast down. "Sat Sri Akal," she whispered.

Jenkins recognized it as a common Sikh greeting. "Yes, indeed." He cleared his throat. "Well, Mrs. Singh—"

"Yes, I know," she interrupted in Urdu. "You want to express some condolence, some sadness. Isn't that so?" She looked up at him, the veil fell away, and Jenkins saw that she was not as plain as he'd imagined. Her eyes were extraordinary, accusing, ablaze in the curtained room.

"He was a good man," Jenkins said, wanting those eyes to stay on him, to punish him.

She smiled. "You're better than him."

"Am I?"

Jenkins didn't know what she meant but it occurred to

him—with a certain horror—that this woman was not grieving. Not at all. That she had none of the weight, none of the blankness of grief. But there was something in her eyes, something more delicate.

"He'd managed to leave the fields," she began, looking past him. "He was proud of that. He was afraid, after the accident, that he wouldn't pass the physical."

"An accident?" Jenkins's voice faltered. "I never noticed."

Her eyes darted back to him. "You're lying. It was obvious. His arm was never the same. He could hardly raise it past his shoulder." She smiled faintly. "Believe me, I know."

It was then that Jenkins noticed the slight bruise on the side of her face. He smiled back despite the pain that shot through his spine. "No, not a thing." He looked beyond her, at the fan, and it seemed to him a murderous thing. A thing that would go on and on, revolving through all of time, slicing through everything that was ever dear to him.

"Cruelty's a strange thing," she said after a long moment. "It gets so you actually miss it."

Her eyes drifted toward the window. It was curtained against the heat, and Jenkins became acutely aware—even though they were behind him—of the tawdriness of these curtains. He felt old. And he felt that some understanding had eluded him; that if life had ever had any nobility it had most certainly, and most perversely, passed him by.

She rose to go, pulling her veil close around her shoulders.

Jenkins wanted to see her out but all he could manage was to rise slightly from his chair.

She turned at the door. "Did he say anything before he died?"

"Your name."

It was a lie she forgave, it seemed to him, and very nearly expected. Once she'd left he drew the curtain back. He watched the two figures—hers straight and determined, her white veil blowing in the hot desert wind, and the old man's bent, weakened, as if the land and the woman beside him were too vast, and had stolen his strength—as they walked toward the outskirts of town. And the horizon, already white with midday heat, seemed just another thin cloth that she could, if she chose, pull like a veil across her face.

Unleashed

The doorman found me the next morning, a Saturday. Just before he did, I was dreaming. I was dreaming that my little sister, Meena, was shaking me awake. "Wake up," she was saying. "We'll be late for school."

We were both adults in the dream, but what she was saying seemed to have a certain logic to it. "I thought this was summer vacation," I said.

It *was* summer in New York, when the doorman found me. I was in the elevator. I suppose I'd been there all night. Or at least, whatever part of the night remained after I got back from the party. Meena and my husband, Vikram, had been there, but I left without telling them. I couldn't remember much more of the party, only that I felt old. Not older than the other people at the party, just old.

I blinked my eyes open, having lost the last part of my dream, and the doorman—I'd passed him in the lobby for months (Vikram had actually chatted with him once and found out he'd lived in India many years ago)—smiled shyly and said in a perfect British accent, "Nine B, isn't it?" And though I was embarrassed, and everything Meena had done came back to me in a rush of pain, it felt like a small kindness: the doorman's brevity, his not saying anything about my being sprawled out on the floor of the elevator, stinking of alcohol, my mouth cottony and rank with stale whiskey. He led me to my door, waited till I found my key, and then stepped aside. "If you need anything else," he said.

I nodded quickly, not meeting his eyes.

By then my head was swimming, and I felt something coming up my throat. I lurched inside and raced to the bathroom. I had never had more than a glass of wine with dinner, maybe two, but after the party I hailed a taxi back to the apartment, saw the round neon sign for Dive 75, and lost count of the number of whiskey sours. I don't even know what came out first in the bathroom: bile or tears. I gripped the toilet seat, sobbing, then sat back against the wall and that's when it came to me, the last part of my dream: "But it's summer vacation," I said. And Meena, just like that, just as if she hadn't slept with my husband, said, "It doesn't matter, Anju. You have to wake up, anyway."

When Meena and I were in elementary school, me in sixth grade and she in third, our family moved to the United States. Our father got a job teaching in Albany, New York. We stood outside our house that first winter, laughing at each snowflake that landed on us. "Look." Meena giggled, pointing to my head. "You have more dandruff than Dad." I shook my head free of snowflakes, glanced down at my hands, and realized I could no longer feel them. Or my toes. I'd never known such cold in India, and it had never occurred to me that cold could do such a thing: crawl into you, as a thief into a house, and steal your fingers and then your toes.

I saw the doorman again the following Monday morning. When I hesitated, he seemed to understand. "I won't tell him," he said, and the firmness and melancholy in his voice felt as if someone had pulled me ashore after a long time at sea.

"I don't know your name."

"Jenkins."

I stood there, fussing with the latch on my purse. I wanted to explain to Jenkins about Vikram, how he'd told me he loved me by the boathouse in Central Park, with the springtime leaves unfurling around us like flags, and how, when he'd asked me to marry him, Amma had breathed, "A cardiologist!" and how all that delight so suddenly had gone sour, like curdling milk.

"My husband tells me you lived in India," I said.

Jenkins smiled. "A long time ago."

"When?"

"During Partition."

"But that was forty years ago! You must hardly remember a thing."

He smiled again, and this time the smile was slow and patient, as if he'd spent years considering that exact statement, and then he said, "On the contrary, my dear, I remember everything."

Behind our house in Albany was a creek, and beyond that creek lived the Finleys. They had one son, Sean, who was older than me and Meena. All that first summer after we moved to New York, we played along the creek. We built dams and made paper sailboats and played cowboys and Indians. "You have to be the Indians," Sean said, "obviously."

Meena and I looked at each other.

He handed us some sticks. "Here's some arrows," he said, holstering a toy pistol in his belt.

"That's not fair," Meena said. "How come you get a gun and we only have arrows?"

Sean sighed loudly. "That's how it was. Don't you even know your own history?"

"I don't think we're those kind of Indians," I said.

"Doesn't matter any to me," Sean said, "you still can't have the gun."

One late afternoon, we played cowboys and Indians, and Sean killed Meena when she jumped from behind one tree to the next, and he killed me while I was hiding behind a huckleberry bush. Afterward he walked triumphantly along the perimeter of the yard and the creek and then we all lay down in the tall grass. The leaves of the birch trees that lined our yard swayed in the breeze and the sun dappled us with coins of light. In the air was the scent of honeysuckle and birch sap and wild lavender. We'd been in America for eight months now, and the sky, as I gazed up at it, no longer felt new to me but shone like polished silver. Here, all the dirt and noise and crowds of India were gone, and we could lie on a wide expanse of grass undisturbed, the sky spinning around us blue and empty and feverish with light.

I was nearly asleep when Sean sat up and said, "I know a new game."

"We have to get home," I said. The sun had dipped low behind the birch trees, and the creek was a dark, silent ribbon.

"You'll like it." He got up and walked to the clump of trees. He stood on the far side of one, where we couldn't see him.

Meena looked at me. A distant lawn mower sputtered like a weeping animal in the hush of twilight.

"Come on!" he yelled.

Meena got up first. I followed. His pants and underwear were around his ankles. There it hung, a deflated balloon. We stared at it. "Go ahead," he said. "Put it in your mouth." We stood there unmoving until he took Meena by the wrist and pushed her onto her knees. Then he grabbed the back of her head and pulled her to him. I thought I might cry but why should I cry when Meena wasn't? Then, when she was done, I did the same. It felt rubbery, flimsy, thin, like a second tongue, and then it stiffened and my mouth filled with something warm and acrid. Sean pulled away and I scrambled to my feet. Meena wasn't watching either of us; she was standing by a tree, scraping at its bark. Even from where I was standing I could see that her tiny fingernails were bleeding. I yanked her wrist away and that's when I heard it again: the lawn mower. It filled the hollow of my head like a rush of water, and I said to it, "Stay with me. Go on and on forever. I'll be fine, so long as you're with me."

Two days later I was walking past a group of girls who were standing just beyond my locker. One of them pointed and the other giggled, and the third turned in my direction and said, "You know what you are, Ann-ju?"

It's Anju, I wanted to say, not Ann-ju. Anju. Like *un*-der, like *un*-til, like that book we're reading in English class, *un*-abridged.

But she was smiling for all the world as if she were about to tell me a grand and wondrous secret. She relished each word as she said it: "You're a slut."

I might've smiled. The word was so perfect in its way. *Slut.* It was a wave pounding a shore. It was Sean leaving my mouth. It was the membrane around my heart, tearing.

Funny what only a few years of marriage does, the way it blinds you. I'd leave them together, alone, while I went to pick up milk at Fairway, or a bottle of wine at West Side. "Don't start without me," I'd sing over my shoulder while Meena chopped vegetables and Vikram smiled over his newspaper or his medical journal or his television. "Don't worry, Anju-like-*un*-dulate," he'd say.

It was a joke between us, from the very start. "But it's two syllables," he said on our first date. "How can you mess that up?"

I shrugged. "Friends I've known for years still get it wrong."

"You're a linguist. That must drive you mad."

"I give them a homophone," I said.

"Like what?"

"An 'un' word. Like un-like."

"Or like un-cork," he offered enthusiastically, and then quieter, looking for a long moment into my eyes, "Or like un-believably beautiful."

I laughed. "You're a cornball."

"How un-kind of you," he said.

"Stop."

"What? You're un-impressed?"

We were at Candle Café. Vikram was doing his residency at Lenox Hill, and he'd asked me to pick the restaurant. It was winter, early evening, but already dark. Snow had fallen earlier in the day but now there was only a shimmering stillness. Taxis flashed by the window, people wrapped in scarves and thick coats trudged past, a distant truck rumbled, and yet the stillness was complete. As if the yellow-lit restaurant, our tiny table at its center, the overstuffed warmth of our wool sweaters, and even the bitterness of our coffees formed a supreme and cardinal quiet, like the very center of a storm, and we only had to go on, to simply go *on*, for the stillness to continue.

* * *

The next time the doorman found me—a week after the incident in the elevator—I was sprawled next to the trash bins, in the basement of our building. I didn't mind the stink of rotting food. Nor the concrete floor damp with runoff from the leaky bins. The light directly above was burned out but the other one, at the opposite end of the narrow hall near the elevators, lent me the feeling of being in a cave. Hidden, wounded, savage. This time I remembered exactly how I'd gotten there: I'd been drinking a glass of wine. Well, a bottle. And then another. Vikram had been called to the hospital, a car accident. One of the passengers in a taxi had been carrying a bouquet of flowers and one of the stems—on a hydrangea, maybe—had punctured her heart. "But *how?*" I asked him. He was putting on his shoes. "How should I know?" His eyes scanned the counter for his keys. "Maybe they were going at high speeds."

"But a *stem?*"

"Anything can be a weapon," he said, sighing impatiently, "if you're going fast enough."

"Maybe it was one of those plastic sticks. You know, the ones they use to hold up the plants."

It had been a week since I'd found out about him and Meena. We three had been at the party together. I'd left the room and when I'd come back in, they'd been standing in the opposite corner. A crowd of people separated us but I'd had a clear view of them, though neither had looked up to see me. They'd laughed about something Vikram had whispered in Meena's ear and then—with the sure intimacy of lovers—he'd taken hold of her wrist. Brought it close to him. It had been a slight gesture, tender, and yet its familiarity, its insistence, had been sexual. I knew, then. I had lived for an entire week, knowing.

"Who the fuck cares whether it was a stick or a stem." Vikram was at the door, his coat over his shoulder. He took a long look at me, taking in my pajamas, my uncombed hair, lips stained red with wine. This sudden change in me, over the past week, went unquestioned, unprobed by him, as if he'd lost interest not only in me but also in the basic machinery of marriage. "What does it matter?" He sighed and dropped his head as he opened the door. "Her *heart* is punctured."

I was the one to take Meena to get her first abortion. She'd called me and said, "Anju, I missed it."

"Missed what?" I asked, thinking she was talking about a class. She was in college and I was in graduate school at CUNY.

I picked her up at her dorm. She stepped through the door wearing sunglasses, a straw hat with a bright green band, and her hair in pigtails.

"You look like you're going on a hayride." I didn't know what else to say. My eyes passed over her stomach and up to her face. But she was looking away, out the window. Her shorts crept up her thighs; their earth-brown flesh embarrassed me. I saw her as a man would see her, felt a shudder, a thin and submerged lust, and thought, *How dare you dress like this? Today, of all days.*

When we got to Dobbs Ferry, there was still an hour until her appointment. We bought coffee and sandwiches at a café and drove to a trail along the Hudson where we sat on a bench. Meena drank in silence. I gazed straight ahead at the river. It was thick with summer runoff, and drifted languid and sallow with afternoon heat. "Do you remember that kid?" Meena said after a long silence. "The one who lived behind our house?"

"Who?"

"Sean. Sean something."

"Finley?"

"Yeah. Finley."

"What about him?"

"You remember that day? Behind that tree?"

Yes, I remember, I wanted to say, I remember everything. "No. What day?"

Meena smiled. "I was called a slut till the day I graduated high school. Can you believe it? From third grade all the way to high school."

I couldn't think of what to say. In the distance, on the other shore, was a group of kayakers. They seemed about to push off and I watched them with a keen longing: their colorful kayaks enclosing them, their shouts and laughter as they called to each other. "It got to where I didn't know if I was trying to prove them wrong, or to prove them right." She laughed.

One of the kayakers reached the middle of the river, and the others followed. Tiny waves lapped at the sides of the kayaks.

"Are you afraid?" I asked.

She turned toward me. "Of what?"

And I knew she wasn't afraid. Had she ever *been* afraid? Fear—sometime during that afternoon with Sean Finley—had left her body and settled into mine.

Meena was a sophomore in high school, and I was about to leave for college, when our parents visited friends in Buffalo and left us alone for the weekend. As soon as their car had pulled out of the driveway, Meena smiled and said, "Let's have a party."

I was eighteen, had been accepted for early admission at Dartmouth, and yet I knew Meena would have her way. There was nothing I could say that she wouldn't find a way around. "Come on, Anju, it'll be fun. You can invite that friend you have, what's her name?"

"Celia."

"Yeah. Invite Celia."

"What if Mom and Dad find out?"

Meena stared at me. "Who would tell them?"

By nine o'clock that night, over thirty people were at our house. More carloads seemed to arrive every few minutes.

The kitchen counter filled with bottles of alcohol; one group of freshmen was doing shots in the dining room. A stereo blasted through the rooms, and all the windows were swung open to the warm summer night. Yet, even in the midst of the crowds of people drinking and shouting and sweating, I could smell the loamy, humid scent of the creek. I leaned out the back window. The Finleys had moved long ago but the creek still flowed between our houses, a beguiling, silver thread. Its tinny ramble, cloaked beneath the other night sounds—the crickets and frogs and rustle of birch leaves—felt to me like a greater music than the one coming from the stereo.

"Hey," a voice said behind me. I turned. A boy I recognized from the swim team. "You don't have a blanket or something, do you?" His skin was alabaster, and his light hair and blue eyes haloed in the moonlight.

"Why do you need a blanket?"

"One of the girls is cold."

"It's eighty degrees out."

He smiled mischievously. "We filled a tub with ice. To hold the liquor. She fell in."

I sighed loudly. He followed me to the upstairs linen closet where I handed him a blanket. As he started back down, he called to me, still smiling, "Hey, I know you. Aren't you Anju like un-happy?"

"Fuck off."

People were upstairs too. A clump sprawled on Meena's bed, smoking. Another group congregated around the bathroom door. A girl shrieked and ran past me. On the second floor, the air was still and hot, and the music wailed as if through a long tunnel. I felt strange, as though I were in an unfamiliar house and had to find my way out. I was also dizzy from the beer I'd drunk, and as I walked through the rooms I strained to hear the sounds of the creek. By the time I opened the door to my parents' room, my head throbbed, and the heat pressed against me like a wall.

At first I thought the mounds on the bed were coats. Then I saw movement. I leaned to close the door and that's when a hand reached out and pushed the sheets away. I saw the boy first, a boy from my junior year math class. Below him was Meena. He stirred above her with small grunts, but Meena was turned toward me. Half her face was shadowed by his body but her eyes were alive to me, watching me with an intensity that quieted all other sounds.

Then she smiled a half smile and her hand left the bed and reached toward me.

Neither one of us blinked. I saw the slope of her breast, its glistening peak. The gold granules of her skin, so like mine. As I stared, a stillness settled on me like a blanket. Her hand remained. In her gaze, in her outstretched hand, seemed to be the thing that had eluded me all my life, a gesture of such pale and abiding love—thin as gauze—that I nearly stepped forward and took it.

The moment passed. The boy looked over at me and laughed. Meena punched him in the chest and told him to hurry. I slammed the door shut, terror and disgust rising. My legs quivered as I descended the stairs. In a week I would leave for college. I would never return home to stay. My visits would become shorter and shorter. I would study abroad, in France, and would move then to New York and through a string of lovers and heartaches. But something of that night would always remain.

The next afternoon, after I'd cleaned the house and taken all of the bottles to the curb, Meena woke up, put on a pair of jeans and a T-shirt, and went out. She came back twenty minutes later with an ice-cream cone. I sat watching her. "Did you want one?" she teased.

After she'd flattened the top of the ice cream, she raised the tip of the sugar cone to her mouth and bit into it. Then she sucked the rest of the ice cream out, like marrow.

"You're disgusting," I said.

"How so?"

"The way you eat that ice cream."

She licked a drop of ice cream from the corner of her mouth and smiled. "Are you sure it's the ice cream?"

I stood up and left the room.

I was curled in a hollow between the trash bins as the doorman stood over me. The wall behind me was warm and rough and cool all at once, like sand. After drinking the two bottles of wine, I'd drifted to sleep, dreamed that I was lying on a beach. The dark horizon in the distance pushed against the shivering gray sea. Shards of moonlight rusted and fell away. I could even see myself, marooned on the shore, lit by the white sand like the forgotten lamp of a firefly.

When I blinked my eyes open, Jenkins was shaking me. "Wake up, my dear. This is no place for a lady."

I looked up at him at the word *lady*. I could feel the crusted edges of my lips, my rancid breath, my body bloated with despair. He lifted me to a slumped position. His skin was dry, flaky, like the wings of a butterfly, and his face contorted with the effort of pulling me up. I let go of his arm and leaned against one of the trash bins. I thought: *I've tried to travel so far from Albany, so far from the girl at that party, and yet here I am again, breathing in a loamy, humid scent.*

"Let me take you upstairs," Jenkins said.

I studied his face: his eyes nested in wrinkles, slippery and placental as newborn birds; his sagging cheeks; shattered capillaries wandering across his skin like lost tribes. The forlorn white wisps of his hair reminded me that I had a husband, and that I'd lost him. Jenkins sat down next to me among the trash bins. We sat in silence for a long while. My head felt light, airy, and I closed my eyes to settle it. I supposed it was the scent but I saw the creek again, and Meena's hand reaching toward me. And the fear returned. The fear that maybe it wasn't what I'd imagined all these years. Maybe she'd wanted me to join them; that was all.

"Why is it," I said, "that some people hold us like they do? Whatever they do only makes us love them more. Did you ever know anyone like that?"

"I did, once. In India. In Pakistan now, I suppose."

I grinned. "Maybe we have a gift for it."

He fell silent. I recalled that long before we'd moved to America, years before the afternoon with Sean Finley, when Meena was five and I was eight, we'd been walking home from school and had cut across a stranger's yard. We'd bought snacks at the stall outside our school gates: one rupee's worth of spiced peanuts and fifty paisa for two thick slices of cucumber sprinkled with tangy amchur. Meena had finished her cucumber and was eating the peanuts one by one. "I only want the round ones," she said. "You eat the halves."

"Why can't you eat them?"

"Dimple said they're diseased."

I threw the bitter end of my cucumber on the ground and scooped out a handful of peanuts. "You're both stupid."

We ducked through a stand of lantana and came out onto a sloped ravine choked with camphire and thorny hawthorn bushes. I held the branches with two fingers while Meena passed through. We reached the base of the ravine, a fallow bed of dirt and silt. The dirt kicked up as we walked, griming our white socks with a thick coat of our mother's wrath. We rarely walked along this stretch of ravine, usually staying on the road until our block, where the ravine was flatter and not so wild.

Meena was in front when the three boys came toward us. They must have heard us and come from the backyards of one of the houses. I'd never seen them before, though they weren't much older than me. Two looked like they might have been brothers, with the same slanted forehead and thick features and oily hair, and the third—standing behind the other two—was thin and rakish, holding something I couldn't see.

"Give me that," one of the brothers said, raising an eye toward our cone of peanuts. At this, the rakish boy needled his way between the brothers and now the three were standing in a row and I saw that he was holding a baby bird. It was hardly bigger than a marble, with wet pink skin and a yellow beak. Even from where I was standing I could make out its delicate gray wings and dark, pulsing organs, its thin cry frantic and clipped like a clogged whistle. The boys were entirely blocking the path at the base of the ravine. The only way to get around them was to slip and slide up one side and down the other. I could do it alone, but Meena wasn't fast enough. I was thinking all this as I looked at them, from one to the other, all in a row. The one in the middle was tallest, so their heads peaked, like a greasy triangle, and I almost laughed. I realized I wasn't scared. That realization was like being handed a weapon, like stealing the keys to a cage.

"It's up to you," I said. "Which do you want more?"

The boy in the middle narrowed his eyes. "Which what?"

"The bird or the peanuts?"

He stared at me in disbelief. Then he brought the arm holding the bird imperceptibly closer to his chest and laughed. "Both."

"That's not one of your choices." I stepped forward and closed my hand over his. He jumped back but the bird was very still. Then it began to struggle. I closed my fist tighter. The boy was turning his hand this way and that, trying to wrench it free. The other boys rushed in and tugged at my wrist. I squeezed harder. One of them pushed me. My legs stiffened, grew roots. The bird pressed against our fists. Its tiny wings buckled, and something wet oozed between my fingers. Someone pulled my hair. But I clutched with all my might, held the boy's hand as if it were the last hand I would ever hold.

He let out a sudden loud yelp and sprang back with an "Ow!"

The bird dropped to the ground like a pebble. The boy's palm was bleeding where the bird's beak had pierced it. The bird writhed, then stilled.

We stood like that for a moment and then I stepped over the bird and strode through the column of boys. Meena followed. We walked in silence for some minutes and then, when we were nearly at our house, she said, "You killed it, didn't you?"

I wiped my hand against my skirt and didn't say a word.

"We should go," I heard Jenkins say. "It's getting late."

My eyes were closed. I was still with the bird, the boys, Meena, and the ravine that bound us together like brushwood. I thought of that afternoon, and of everything that had come after, and opened my eyes. I saw a dirty, thin strip of window above the bins, facing an alley. Beyond the window was only a hard brick wall, and I wondered if I could be that girl again. Was defiance temporary, like a gust of wind that lifted you once, then set you down? Or was it always there, inside of you, like a small dinghy tied to the harbor of your heart, waiting, at the ready, to launch?

Night was falling. The wall of the building opposite loomed as the light thinned. A dinghy, I decided. They would have to be asked, I would have to hear. And in due course, steps would have to be taken. But for now, as if each layer of life had its proper place, everything beyond the asking was a blur.

I let Jenkins help me to my feet. We were the same height and something about this detail made me lean over and kiss his cheek. "Let's get married," I said.

He laughed kindly. "Before we do, shouldn't I at least know your name?"

"It's Anju," I said. "Anju, like un-leashed."

Jenkins led me to the elevator. He held my hand, and not until the doors slid open again on the ninth floor did he let go.

BLINDFOLD

Bandra wasn't in the market for a girl but when she saw Zubaida she knew, even with a girl so young, that she would grow up to be beautiful. She had an eye for these things. She asked the driver of the horse cart to stop. "Where are we?" she yelled up to him. "Doran Pur," he said. Bandra stepped out of the cart. The village of Doran Pur was small, just a sprinkling of low, unadorned huts. Farmers and shepherds, Bandra thought. And then she thought, Impoverished. She moved closer to Zubaida to get a better look. The girl was hardly four or five years old; she took no notice of Bandra. She was busy collecting firewood, kindling really, which was all her tiny hands could manage. But she was determined. She broke off branches from trees, the lower ones, the ones she could reach. She scoured the ground for stray pieces. She had a basket tied to her back in which she carefully placed each piece of wood. Bandra watched her with interest, and then turned to look for a mother or a sister. There was no one in sight. When she turned back, Bandra

gasped. The girl had picked up a stick with something hanging. Something moving. It took a moment but then Bandra
saw it: a snake. She nearly yelled out, ran to her, but before
she could, Zubaida calmly picked up the snake behind its
head—gray, with a brown threaded pattern to its scales—
and held it. Its body coiled, its mouth yawned open, hinged
and menacing, its head angled upward. Bandra thought she
would fling it away, but instead the girl turned the snake
around to face her and opened her own mouth wide. What
was she *doing*? Bandra held her breath. Around them was a
stillness, a quiet. Bandra heard the whine of mosquitoes.
She's challenging it, Bandra realized slowly, she's challenging a snake. After a moment, there came a shout from one
of the huts to hurry up and bring the wood, and when the
girl heard it, she tossed the snake into a nearby bush and hurried off toward the village. Bandra watched her, and it was
then that she decided she wanted her for the brothel.

Bandra gave the girl's father a silver coin to hold her, a
down payment of sorts, with a guarantee that he would sell
to Bandra when the girl was older. Eleven was the agreed-
upon age. Four silver coins was the agreed-upon price.

Bandra was thirty years old, or so she guessed. Her mother
had told her that she was born the year of some great Indian
mutiny against the British. That was in 1857, or maybe 1856,
and would put her at thirty or thirty-one. It didn't matter;
she was worn out. She had been married to her husband
when she was twelve. He had been thirty-nine. He had

owned a small plot of land, inherited from his father, but his true wealth had been in the trade of gur, which was sent swaying on the backs of donkeys across the Spin Ghar, through the Khyber Pass, and into Afghanistan. It had been lucrative, but he had gambled it all away. All of it. So that when he'd died, ten years ago, he'd left her the plot of flat, useless land, a mountain of debt, and three young children. She'd stood in the center of this plot of land and had known it could grow nothing—not even a shriveled sprig of cilantro—and so she'd sold everything, her modest pieces of jewelry, all the furniture in the house, livestock, and even her hair, and used the money to build the brothel and buy her first three girls.

Her brothel was a simple affair: tucked into the outskirts of Peshawar, outside the walled city, it was a collection of six mud huts surrounding a central courtyard. Bandra's was the seventh, and the biggest hut. Hers actually had a carved wooden almirah, windows, multiple rooms, and two doors, one that opened onto the courtyard and one that led into the street. The other huts had only one door, facing the courtyard, so that the girls had to pass through Bandra's hut to leave the compound. Though, what reason was there for them to leave? Bandra provided all the food, clothing, and sundries they needed. In fact, they were so fond of her they called her Bandra-ma. Bandra was especially proud of this: that they felt close enough to her to call her ma. There were, of course, times when one or another of them needed a good beating, or she would have to force-feed one of the girls for a few days: the poor things sometimes got it into their heads that starving themselves would allow them to leave the compound. That was not so. Bandra recalled the death of that one sweet girl, what was her name? But that was long ago, and her family, when they'd been told, had merely shrugged.

Seven years passed. Bandra appeared again in Doran Pur, at the door of Zubaida's parents. The father came in with his sheep late that night, and Bandra was waiting inside, sipping a cup of tea. The father, named Abdul Shahid, stopped in his tracks when he saw her. There were other children in the house, but Zubaida was nowhere in sight. "Where is she?" Bandra asked, her voice even.

"Who?"

"Your daughter. The one I bought."

"I don't know. She's run off."

Bandra smiled. "If that were true," she said, "I would have known about it the week *before* she left. That's how close my ears are to the ground. Now, where is she?"

Abdul Shahid shuffled his feet, and finally entered his house. "Tea," he called out to his wife. After a moment, he said, "We don't want to sell." He went to a satchel that was hidden between a pile of blankets. He undid a knot and held out a handful of coins. "Here is your money, with interest."

Bandra looked at the coins. She needed a new girl; she was down to four. Her customers had been dwindling. Besides, a deal was a deal. "You know the most interesting thing about a beautiful girl?" she asked the father.

He stared at her.

"It's that you can't keep her hidden for long." Bandra knocked the coins out of his hand. "Find her," she said.

"No."

Bandra grew suddenly tired. She recalled Zubaida as she'd last seen her, a little girl, hurrying home, unaware of the danger she'd held so easily in her tiny hands. Bandra looked at the father and sighed. She was tired of the cowardice—the utter weakness—of men. She got up to leave.

"What will you do?" the father asked, a slight trembling entering his voice.

"I'm going to recover my investment."

"But I'm returning your money."

"I don't want the money, Abdul Shahid, I want the girl."

He let go of the satchel and lunged toward her. But Bandra was by the door and slipped past him. She was at the boundary of his parched, pitiable land when he called out, "I'll go to the malik."

"Go ahead," she said, "and give him my regards. He's my uncle."

It took Bandra less than a fortnight to find her. She was in the tehsil of Charsadda, at the home of a distant maternal uncle. She knew her at once. And she had to laugh: Zubaida was playing *outside* when she arrived. Bandra simply walked up to her, grabbed her by the hair, and dragged her into the waiting donkey cart. Zubaida screamed and screamed, and a few women and small children came to the door, but no one helped her. See, Bandra thought, women have more sense. Still, it was difficult getting Zubaida into the cart. She kicked and punched and pulled. She bit. At one point, in the twenty steps it took to reach the donkey cart, Zubaida yanked so hard that she left Bandra holding only a tuft of hair. She ran as fast as a tiny panther and Bandra had to tackle her from behind and pin her to the ground before she stopped squirming. When she finally got her into the cart, Bandra tied her hands and feet together with one long piece of rope, then bound that rope around her own waist. She stuffed a cloth into Zubaida's mouth. She waited a few minutes till she got her breath back then Bandra looked at her new purchase. The girl's hair was in disarray. There were cuts and bruises on her arms and face, with a substantial gash on her cheek. Her clothes were ripped. She tugged at the rope around her feet and wrists, bellowed against the cloth in her mouth, shot daggers at Bandra with her eyes. But Bandra smiled, because she had been right: Zubaida was indeed beautiful.

They rode through the countryside nearing Peshawar. It was a dry September, the land was a veil of dust, rising and falling with the wind. There were tiny fields here and there, in the distance, like paratha drying in the sun, but otherwise there was a wide and singing emptiness. The donkey cart was covered, and it rocked gently. Bandra dozed. Now that she'd found Zubaida, she'd have to send some men to teach her father a lesson. It was annoying, but necessary. Word traveled, and if even one father got away with it, she would lose all credibility. A deal, after all, was a deal. She thought about sending him the remaining three silver coins she owed for Zubaida but she decided against it: she'd use it to cover the cost and aggravation of finding her. Bandra yawned. Then she started thinking about her three children. She had two boys and a girl. The girl was with her grandmother in Nowshera. The two boys were in a British school in Rawalpindi. She obviously couldn't raise them in the brothel, but she suspected there was something more to their distance. When she visited them, they were cold toward her, as if they didn't know her, as if she were a distant relative they were forced to be affectionate toward. "I'm your mother," Bandra said to them once, "remember me?" The younger boy, twelve years old at the time, said, "No." The older boy shrugged. She had even less luck with her daughter. She was the youngest, eleven, and when Bandra visited her the girl turned away and walked out of the room. "Ma," Bandra had asked, "why, why won't they come to me?" And her mother, cryptically, had said, "What is there to come to? You're a fog, a mist."

A fog, a mist? What did they know, Bandra thought angrily, they were kept in nice clothes and the best schools without lifting a finger. She looked out of the opening in the cart and saw low hills in the distance. They were blue, shadowed at sundown. Next to the cart was a lone tree and a bird flew onto one of its branches. Then another. Soon, before the tree receded away, there was a row of birds. Chirping, but mostly silent. Watching. What did they see? Bandra wondered. A cart. A tied-up girl. A fog, a mist.

She closed her eyes.

When they arrived at the compound, Gulshan was waiting for them. She was not Bandra's favorite, but she had been here the longest, since she was eight; she was now fourteen. The men liked her well enough, she had the eyes and the lips of a child, but she lacked something. Maybe it was sense, Bandra sometimes thought, or maybe it was daring. She had some regulars because they could do with her what they wanted; she was compliant. Her utter obedience was not at all surprising: Bandra had found her dirty and covered in lice in a hovel in Wazir Bagh, her father had beat her every day, and there had been so little food in the family that when Bandra had given her her first meal in the brothel of dry roti and a bit of dal, Gulshan had fallen to her knees and wept.

"Bandra-ma," Gulshan began as soon as they entered the courtyard, "Siddiqah started her monthly, during, you know, and now the customer refuses to leave. He wants a refund."

"Where is he?"

"In the sitting room." The sitting room was in Bandra's hut, where the customers entered and paid.

"She's early," Bandra said, to no one in particular. Then she looked at Zubaida. She just stood there, blinking, the cloth still stuffed into her mouth, her wrists and ankles still bound. She untied the rope at her waist. "Take her to the green door," she told Gulshan.

It was not really a door, just a curtain, but each girl had a different color. Gulshan's was red. Siddiqah's was blue. And Zubaida's would be green. There were of course wooden doors behind the curtains, but the colors made it easier for the customers. Bandra watched her hop away, being led by Gulshan. How odd, she thought, that she was suddenly so docile. It was surprising, but it always came, eventually: the acceptance that this would be their life, and that whatever had come before was of no consequence: the love of a mother, the cradle of a lap, the laughter of siblings, the one cup of evening tea passed from hand to hand, the long and wistful evenings watching a far horizon. To this end, Bandra had insisted, when the compound was built, that none of their rooms have windows.

She turned and walked to her sitting room, the customer was waiting.

Bandra let a few days pass, Zubaida's cuts and bruises needed to heal. The men, *they* wanted to be the ones to make them. She fed her well: two rotis a day, plenty of dal, the choicest pieces of mutton. She was a little on the thin side, which was typical of girls from the countryside. But with each passing day, Zubaida grew plumper, her skin regained its flawlessness, her hair, oiled and combed, shone like moonlight. It was only her docility that bothered Bandra. She didn't trust it. It was too complete. And another thing: she refused to call her Bandra-ma. She didn't call her anything. She hardly spoke. In fact, she never actually addressed Bandra or any of the other girls directly. She whispered, every now and then, and only with Gulshan.

"What does she say to you?" Bandra asked.

"She asks questions."

"Like what?"

"Like, why are we here? Why don't we have windows? Why did that lady buy me? Why can't we go outside? Things like that."

Bandra smiled and said nothing.

After two weeks, she dressed Zubaida in various clothes until she found the right ones. Gulabi was her color. She drew a thick line of kohl around her eyes and painted her skin with henna. Bandra stood back. The blouse was low cut but not overly revealing. The girl had small breasts, no larger than a baby chikoo but that made no difference; men liked the suggestion of childhood. She grabbed Zubaida by the chin, hoisted her face up to meet her eyes, and said, "Your name is now Layla. Don't forget." Then she sent for her oldest and most regular customer, Abdul Kareem. He was forty-eight, a well-to-do wheat merchant, and he had paid extra for the virgin. When he came in she could see the lust dancing in his eyes.

"What's her name?" he asked.

"Layla."

"Ah." He sighed. "Just like in the lover's tale."

"Yes," Bandra said, "just like that."

She hadn't told Layla what to expect. It was better not to. She waited outside, as she always did with her new girls. At first she heard tussling. Later there were screams, the girl's, followed by low grunts. Then a loud thump before it went quiet. When Abdul Kareem came out of her room, he and Bandra went straight to her sitting room. "Feisty." He smiled. Bandra looked at his face and saw scratches on his neck and chin. He showed her a bite mark on his arm. Bandra was apologetic but Abdul Kareem said, "Oh no, oh no, you should charge extra." After that, the stream of customers for Layla was steady. Six, seven a day. Bandra watched her carefully. She was still obedient, eating only what was given her, speaking only with Gulshan, but on some mornings Bandra noticed that her eyes were red. She once spied mysterious burn marks on her ankles. One evening she handed her a knife, the curved one attached to a flat wooden base, to cut vegetables and Layla reached for it and then she stared at it. And then, for the first time, she smiled. After that, Bandra instructed Gulshan to keep all sharp objects away from Layla. She stripped her room down to its barest: a cot stuffed with straw, a wool blanket, a cushion for the customers, a wooden hook by the door, to hold the men's caftans, and a chamberstick for the candle. She took the candle. But she left a small decorative rug on the wall. It was pretty, and after all, what harm could it do?

Two years went by. The number of customers for Layla only increased. She was busy from early afternoon to late at night. Sometimes with two or three at the same time. Even if Bandra had given her father the remaining coins, she would have made it back many times over. She was pleased, and even though Layla still only spoke one or two words to her, Gulshan passed on whatever there was to know. And once, Abdul Kareem, who now requested Layla at least three times a week, said to Bandra, "She kept repeating the same name, over and over again."

"What name?"

"The name Zubaida," he said, perplexed. "Who is Zubaida?"

Bandra looked away. "No one," she said.

At dinner that night, Bandra grabbed Layla's hand as she reached for the roti. "I told you," she said, "your name is Layla. Did you forget?" Their eyes met. The other girls stopped eating. Layla looked at her, a glint of melancholy, near sadness, coloring them for an instant. Then she closed them, slowly, as if she was struggling with something— something indescribably painful—and when she opened them, she took her free hand, her left, and flipped her plate over. The plate, piled high with brinjal and potato curry, clattered against Siddiqah's plate. It rolled to a stop in a far corner. Bits of curry spewed across the floor and down the opposite wall. It dripped down their clothes, their hair. Bandra yanked Layla up by the arm and dragged her to the almirah. She pushed her inside. To fit in the wardrobe, Layla had to pull her knees to her chest, crumple her body into a tight ball. Bandra locked the door and left her there till morning.

Two or three weeks after that incident, just before daybreak, Bandra was walking through the courtyard when she heard a sound. She stopped. It was summertime, and the heat was scorching. Waves of hot air, thick as walls, streamed in from the valleys. Only the early mornings were cool, and so she'd gotten up in the dark to bathe. She stood in the courtyard and listened. The sound was coming from Layla's room. She tiptoed closer. It was Layla; she was talking. It was only a hush, a whisper, but it was definitely her voice. Bandra leaned in. The door was open, for a breeze, with only the curtain pulled across it. She could hardly hear but it sounded like she was having a conversation with someone. But who? Bandra yanked the green curtain aside. At first only darkness. Then, in a far corner, Layla huddled on her cot.

"Who were you talking to?"

Layla glared at her.

"Who?"

She said nothing. Bandra saw that her hands were behind her back, against the wall. She took two steps, crossed the room, and wrenched her hands out so she could see them. What was that? A scrap. A tiny piece of roti.

"I was hungry," she said.

"You get plenty at dinner." Bandra took the morsel of roti, hardly bigger than her fingertip, and left the room.

She enlisted Gulshan. "Find out who she's talking to," she said. "Early in the morning, and in this heat. Maybe only to herself, but find out."

It took her hardly a day. That evening she told Bandra, "A mouse."

"A mouse?"

"It lives with her. In her bed. In the straw."

Bandra was baffled. She said, "What could she possibly have to say to a mouse?"

"She says it's her only friend."

Bandra shook her head. It was disgusting, and besides, she should be sleeping, not staying up all night *talking* to a mouse. And what was that she was feeling? Envy? Over a mouse? It was ridiculous. She brushed the thought aside. It took her a few days but one evening she found the neighborhood cat, lured it into Layla's room when she went to bathe, and closed the door. She asked Layla for help in the kitchen when she returned. She kept her busy: cleaning the main hut, sweeping the courtyard, mending clothes. Then she suggested all the girls sleep in the sitting room. They stared at each other in disbelief. Bandra made it known that she preferred sleeping alone, and she always padlocked both doors leading from her quarters—the door opening onto the street and the one to the courtyard—keeping the keys to the padlocks tied to the pull string of her kurta bottom. But this evening she said, "It's cooler in here," and invited them to stay. She set out bowls of water at the open windows and courtyard door to cool the room further. When they woke in the morning the girls plodded back to their rooms, evenly, in a straight line. Bandra waited inside. She heard laughter, something Siddiqah had said, and then there was quiet. A cat darted past her. And then came the scream: the one she knew would come.

Bandra took a strange, disproportionate pleasure in imagining the mouse's shredded body. Its slippery entrails, shining like the insides of fruit. Tiny tufts of white hair, strewn around the room like miniature clumps of mountain grass. She expected anger, rage, weeping, or perhaps even a greater stoicism from Layla, but instead, later in the morning, before the customers began to arrive, she emerged from her room and stood at the door.

"Bandra-ma," she said.

Bandra looked up, astonished. "What is it?"

"I need a pail and a rag, Bandra-ma."

"Oh? What happened?"

"Nothing. I just want to clean the floor and the walls."

"Why?"

"A cat got in last night. And you know how cats are."

What was she playing at, Bandra wondered. And why was she being so sweet? She had never once, in the two years she'd been here, called her Bandra-ma. And *now*? She was suspicious, but she lent her the pail and rags and kept a close watch on her for the next few days. Nothing happened. She only grew sweeter. Day by day, week by week, until, one day, Bandra stopped watching her.

The months passed. Layla no longer confided in Gulshan. That, of course, was to be expected. Bandra realized that their friendship had been a source of information, and that she'd lost a link that had been instrumental, but it had been worth it, she decided. Layla was tame. Still, other things, peculiar things, began to happen. Nothing alarming but just things that gave Bandra pause. The wooden hook, for example, the one in Layla's room meant to hold the men's caftans, broke off.

"It broke off?" Bandra asked. "How?"

"I don't know, Bandra-ma," Layla said. "It just did."

"Then where is it?" Bandra said, looking at the jagged stump that remained stuck in the wall.

"The man took it."

"He took it? *Why?*"

Layla shrugged. "How should I know," she said.

Bandra looked around the room: the cot, the cushion, the rug hanging on the wall. All of these were in place. So she shook her head, puzzled, and had the hook replaced.

Soon after, winter arrived. They shivered and built fires in the courtyard. They sat huddled in thick shawls. The girls, in their windowless rooms, waited for spring. What they couldn't see were the foothills white with snow then brown with moisture then green with new spring grass. When the air turned warm, after long months, and swept into the courtyard, they were delighted. Bandra believed in none of the romance of spring, but the scented air loosened her limbs, made her more generous than she was in other seasons. So that when Abdul Kareem came to her and requested more straw, she smiled and said, "What for?"

"The girl's bed," he said, "it's lumpy."

"Lumpy? But it was refilled just last year."

"My knees hurt."

"Then lie on your back, old man." Bandra laughed. "Let her do the work."

Nevertheless, she ordered a bale of straw and had all the cots stuffed to capacity. But when autumn came, Abdul Kareem brought it up again. He said, "I thought you were going to have them stuffed?"

She looked at Abdul Kareem for a long moment, longer than she'd intended, and said, "I did."

The following winter, Gulshan got sick. She was pregnant by one of the men. Bandra was used to this, it had happened twice before. She gave her herbs, the same ones she'd given the other girls, but Gulshan reacted badly. At first, she retched and retched, just as the others had. She was nauseated. She stayed in bed, screaming in pain. Bandra couldn't understand it: for the others, it had been over in three or four days, but with Gulshan, it only got worse. Two weeks passed. She was faint with hunger, delirious with pain. Then she began to bleed. There seemed no end to the blood. "Call the doctor," Siddiqah cried. The other girls turned away. Layla stood silently. Bandra refused. "She'll be fine," she said. Layla looked at her and walked out of the room.

They took turns watching her. One night, while Bandra was at her bedside, Gulshan sat straight up on her cot and smiled. Her eyes were mad. She looked around the room with an ineffable pleasure, as though it were a room from a childhood she did not have, then she picked up the sheet— soaked in blood—that was between her legs and held it tight against her bosom. "Roses." She sighed.

You fool, Bandra thought, as if you've ever held a rose.

The next morning she was dead.

When Layla was fifteen, Abdul Kareem came to see Bandra again. He was fifty-two but he sat on the cushion as shy and squirming as a little boy. Bandra served him tea. He still said nothing.

"What is it, Abdul Kareem?"

"I want to marry her," he said.

Bandra knew exactly whom he meant. "It will cost you," she said.

"I have money."

"You can't marry a randi," she protested mildly. "You'll never be able to raise your head again."

"Then I'll keep her."

They decided on a price. It was twenty times what Bandra had paid for her. She could buy *ten* new girls with that money. Bandra could hardly believe her luck; she counted and recounted the money and laughed. The other arrangements too were conducted as if it were a wedding. Abdul Kareem sent more money for Layla's trousseau, and he requested that Bandra apply uptan on the night before she was to leave the brothel. It's all a rich man's whim, Bandra thought. As for the trousseau, she kept half the money and with the other half, she bought cheap silks and thin cotton underclothes. She placed them all in a trunk in her sitting room, lest the other girls take them during the night.

The day before Layla was scheduled to leave, the compound was bustling. As instructed, Bandra applied the uptan. All the girls bathed and dressed in their best clothes; none of them worked. They played games in the courtyard, and teased each other like schoolgirls. Abdul Kareem sent sweets, which made them squeal, and they ate them all afternoon with relish. That evening they had a meal of mutton, and capsicum curry, and paratha lathered with ghee. Siddiqah lay on the cushion in the sitting room, groaning with stomach pain from all the sweets and rich food. Bandra told her to go to bed. One by one all the girls left, except Layla. She walked over to the trunk full of clothes and touched its edges.

"This is all for me?" she asked.

"That's right," Bandra said, dozing.

She opened the squeaking lid of the trunk and looked inside. She turned and said, "Bandra-ma?"

"Yes?"

"May I sleep here tonight?"

"Why do you want to do that?"

"It's my last night."

Bandra agreed, yawning. She was asleep almost as soon as Layla blew out the candle. But just before she did, Bandra saw that the lid of the trunk was still open. She thought she should ask her to close it, but she didn't.

It was nearly morning when Bandra felt a gentle waft of wind against her feet. It was so soft; it tickled. She rubbed her feet together in her sleep and smiled, slightly, as if she were dreaming. Then there was another breeze (she thought she'd closed the window) but this time, it blew the other way, though it was just as lovely, like feathers. She was playing in this wind; she heard it rustle the leaves of the trees. They danced gaily, just for her. But then the branches swung low and scraped against her ankles. Cut into them. The branches of what trees? That's what she asked herself in her dream, what trees?

Then her eyes shot open.

The moment they did, someone stuffed a rag into her mouth. Bandra gagged. A shadow passed over her. She bucked forward. Her arms flailed. It was too dark to see the intruder; the window was closed. Her eyes blurred. Focus, she told herself. She tried to get up but her ankles were bound. It was as if her feet had fused in the night. She tilted her head to look down and see what held them but by then someone came from behind, yanked up her arms, and tied them roughly, trussing at the wrists so that her fingers tingled. Bandra thrashed. She flopped onto her stomach. Who was it? She blew against the rag in her mouth, blew hard, but it stayed in place. The intruder turned her over again with a kick to her stomach. She groaned in pain. And then, only then, did she see who it was. And only because she wanted her to.

It was Layla.

She looked down at Bandra. Her face in the half-light was motionless. Eerie in its beauty. She left the room. Bandra crawled and kicked toward the door. Slithered like a snake. She'd hardly moved a yard or two when Layla came back. She had the curved knife in her hand, the one shaped like a scimitar, and Bandra thought she might slit her throat. But instead, Layla bent down, shoved a knee into her chest, and thrust Bandra's head to the side. Out of the corner of her eye she saw the wooden base of the knife coming toward her. In the next instant, it rammed into her face. Rush of pain. A blurred hand reached out. Then the knife came down again.

Teeth flew out.

As Bandra lay groaning, Layla snipped the keys from her kurta bottom, opened the door leading to the street, and let in the morning light. And as if in a dream, the dream that Bandra had just left, Layla turned toward her, and she said, "My name is Zubaida."

Bandra was found, not much later. The swelling and pain in her face took weeks to subside. Her tongue, when she was finally able to move it, groped for teeth and found only three. And what had been used to bind her hands and feet, Bandra was told, were the cheap silks she had bought for Zubaida's trousseau. She almost laughed. Then she saw herself as if from above, bound: her legs, her hands, her mouth. She saw the cart, the fog, the mist. And then she did laugh.

It was another two weeks or so before Fawzi, the man who did odd jobs in the neighborhood, came by and said he had mud left over from another job and would she like the hole plugged up.

"What hole?" Bandra asked.

"The one in your wall."

She followed him to the outside of the compound and saw that there was indeed a hole. It was stuffed with straw. She couldn't imagine why there was a hole, or where it had come from. She estimated it was in Zubaida's old room. When she went around, to the other side, there was no hole. How could that be? She looked at every inch of the outside wall until her eyes finally traveled to the decorative rug. She was shaking—with anger, with fear—as she reached for it. She ripped it off the wall and there it was: a hole. Except Fawzi had been wrong. This was not just any hole. It was not ill formed, or sloppy, or small. It was not desperate, and it was not careless. It was planned. It was a window.

She punched through the straw. Her arms were frenzied, she was crying and somehow laughing all at once. The hook, she thought, the wooden hook. I'm a fool! By the time she punched through all of it, the straw was in her hair and in her clothes and it filled her nose. And once it all came down, in poured light.

Over the course of the next two decades, Bandra's business suffered. A new brothel was opened. It catered mainly to the British officers in the nearby cantonments. Alcohol was served. Bandra disapproved. She was forced to reduce her rates, but even the day laborers saved up and went to the new brothel, or they picked up a woman on the street, which was even cheaper.

In her old age Bandra wandered the streets of Peshawar. She wandered from the outdoor markets to the mosque then to Ghanta Ghar and then back again. She had no money, and only rarely made a pittance helping to deliver babies, especially girl babies that needed to be disposed of. She was eighty now. Or was she ninety? Little boys laughed at her, and threw rotten fruit when she passed them on the streets. They taunted her. But she paid them no mind. Her thoughts were elsewhere. They were in another time, and in another place. And of all the girls, she thought most often of Zubaida. Where had she gone? Did she too wander the streets? What else could a girl of fifteen, alone, impure, unable to return home, have done?

In her wanderings she sometimes stopped at various stalls and begged for food. Vegetables they were throwing out because they were spoiled, or day-old roti they might be able to spare. Once she happened upon a man who had a monkey. The monkey was doing tricks. The trainer was seated in front of it, telling the monkey what to do: somersaults, jumping rope, running and climbing. People laughed when the monkey bared its teeth and stuck out its tongue. The whole time, the monkey was blindfolded. Bandra waited until the show was over. Until all the spectators had left. "Why is it blindfolded?" she asked.

The trainer sat back, studied her, and she could see the disgust in his eyes. An old woman, a beggar. Her clothes dirty, smelling, her body bent and wrinkled, a mouth with hardly any teeth. He looked away. "Why? Are you its mother?"

Bandra said nothing.

The man collected the few copper coins people had

thrown into his topee. He counted them slowly then put them into an inside pocket. He began packing up the few props that had been used.

"Why?" she asked again.

The man turned toward her. She thought of the snake, the one Zubaida had challenged. She thought of her as a little girl, collecting kindling, hurrying home to an evening fire. The man held the topee toward her. "Throw in a coin or get out," he bellowed.

Bandra remained, watching him.

When he had finished packing up, the monkey climbed onto his shoulder. The blindfold was still in place. The trainer rose to go, he looked at Bandra and shook his head. She thought he might yell at her again, as they so often did, but he only raised his voice. "It's a trick," he said. "If you can get them to keep the blindfold on and think it's dark, even when it's not, you make them afraid. And if you make them afraid," he said, "you make them yours."

THE LOST RIBBON

If I were to tell Leela what I'd done, I know what she'd say. She'd say, No mother would do that. No mother could do that. But then I look down at my arm, at the scar left by the cigarette burn, and think, What do you know? Because what *I* know, what I won't tell her, but what I will tell you now, is that I was long dead before I ever killed you.

Yet it's all true: I took you, your moist eyelashes wide with curiosity, the tiny yellow ribbon in your fine hair bowed and alert, watchful, as if it were standing guard, and I wrapped my hands around your neck. You blinked. Then you smiled your toothless smile. It was a hot, bright morning in September. The sun shoved through the cracks in the door, past the edges of the curtains. Everyone said it was a long and strange summer. The days too warm, the clouds too thin. The monsoons were so late that year that well into September the entire Punjab and the Northwest Frontier broiled, simmered indecently, the dust a mad dervish, crawling into even your earlobes in the long breathless nights.

I'd bathed you that morning using more water than usual. I sprinkled your tender skin with a thick coating of talcum powder to protect you from the heat. I dressed you in a freshly laundered bright pink frock. I'd spread it carefully under a thick bundle of clothes the night before to press it, to make sure the pleats were crisp. I'd picked the yellow ribbon because it was the closest color to white. But none of it mattered. Thousands upon thousands were dying that summer. Entire villages were being laid waste in the crossings between India and Pakistan. What did it matter if the ribbon was yellow or white? I tightened my grip, I willed myself to close my eyes, to keep pressing. I felt the gentle curve of your windpipe, your brave and rumpled pulse, and I told myself, If you don't kill her, he will.

The only question I ask myself now, after all these years, is why I closed my eyes. Why? I missed the last tiny breaths of the only life I've ever loved. There are so many answers, or maybe there are none. But I was afraid; I was afraid you'd recognize the act. *Know* what I was doing. And in some small corner of your silvery, still-beating six-week-old heart, you'd scoff at me. You'd say, What makes you think I couldn't have withstood the world? And I would've laughed and said, It's not the world we have to withstand, my Noora, it is ourselves.

But all of that is ridiculous, of course. You hadn't spoken a word. How could you? Only the tiny yellow ribbon seemed capable still of speech, still upright, oblivious, delighted by the fineness of your hair, by the life it would never lead.

Besides, I know what you would've said if you could've formed the words. You would've said exactly the same thing he said the first time he raped me. You would've said, Open your eyes.

It's funny though, the things we suffer and the things we remember about that suffering. It's almost as though our thoughts were pebbles skipping across a pond. Take, for instance, that first time. I was fourteen. Now, when I think on that night, think of him pushing up my lehenga, smothering my face with his free hand, stuffing his fingers into my mouth to muffle my screams, I think of your grandmother's paneer. It's just a flash, really, but the softness of the cheese, the taste of the woodsmoke and the twilight in which they were prepared, the thin gold filigree of the cube of paneer breaking like skin, they all rush through me in this moment as if I were that pebble, flying through the air. Then I hit the water again, and something is pushing into me. Thin and hard and knife-edged, it pushed, pushed, until I cried out. Then I think of something else, something quite ordinary, like how cold my feet are in the winter. Or maybe how I should bring in the clothesline; it looks like rain. That's how memory works, skips like a happy pebble, even if the memory is so very far from happy.

Imagine if we remembered things exactly as they happened. If the pebble just glided along the surface. Then we'd remember every detail. One after another after another. So imagine: after that first time, a slight sucking sound and then he turned over and went to sleep. I lay next to him, too afraid to move. There was something warm trickling between my legs and when I reached down my hand came up bloody. But what made me wince was the awful tenderness. That whole part of my body, below my waist, seemed quite apart from me. A scared and collapsed and quivering animal, curled into a ball, knowing only one thing: that nothing remained. Nothing. Nothing would come after. Nothing had come before. He began to snore, lightly, and the room felt close and thick and seething, the smell of his pungent underclothes hung in the air. I rose quietly, my legs nearly buckling under my new and awful weight. The door was padlocked from the inside but the small window was thrown open. That was when I saw the stars.

They were horrible: those stars.

I thought then of a ribbon I'd worn as a child. It was white with a beautiful tendril of red and gold threaded along both edges. I adored that ribbon. It seemed to me the height of loveliness. I wore it to school sparingly, only on Saturdays. I washed and dried it myself, then ironed it delicately with a brass tumbler full of hot water. Then I rolled it up neatly, with extraordinary care, and placed it under my pillow until the next Saturday. And it was during one of those Saturdays, after our half day of school, that a girl in my class—she was the prettiest of all of us—snapped up the ribbon when it'd untwined from my braid. She waved it in front of me teasingly and laughed. I tried to grab it but she ran off down the street. I chased after her. Already, tears stung my eyes so I could hardly see. I saw only her blurred figure, weaving in and out of the narrow alleys. Our town, just outside of Calcutta, was not very big; its great moment had come when Pandit Nehru had traveled through on a Delhi-bound train. My father had taken me to the station, raised me onto his shoulders, and as the train had sped past he'd pointed to one of the windows, and in the midst of the roar of the gathered crowd he'd yelled, "See him? There! There! *He* is our father." I wanted to say, But I thought you were my father, but even from above I saw his beaming face and decided against it.

Instead I watched the thin trail of smoke disappearing westward into deepest Bengal. It looked like the ribbon I'd so recently lost. I gave chase for over an hour. She'd held it up the entire time, the white ribbon streaming and bobbing in the wind like a kite, like the long tail of a shining mystical bird. I followed it until the girl disappeared down a small alleyway. But when I turned into it she was gone. She'd probably ducked inside one of the homes, probably her own, and I was left standing, alone, lost, but before the fear overtook me—in the tiny moment before I began to cry—I had the strangest thought. I looked around me at the close alley and the unfamiliar houses, asleep in the silence of the afternoon, and in that silence I heard my heart beating. It was a quick and steady beating, a fluttering, and I thought, It's the bird, it's left me with its heart. And though I've lost its tail I haven't, I have not, lost its heart.

But on that night, at that window, looking at those horrible stars, I knew I'd lost both.

So you see? It's no good. The pebble *must* skip. Otherwise we'd die a thousand deaths before we got through a single day.

I'm an old woman now. I've been living in this government-run hostel for single women, near Khalsa College on Grand Trunk Road, for over forty years. Most of the girls living in the hostel are students at the college. They are all so beautiful, these girls. Their faces are clear, bright with plans for the future; I can hear them giggling as they tease each other about the boys in their classes or swoon over the newest film hero. They'll be gone in a year or two, married off to pleasant boys, and they will take up a job, have children, they will settle into the many small and sweet intricacies of family life, and I will still be here. Sometimes, in the mess hall, I sit in the same far corner I have sat in for many, many years and stare at their resplendent faces. What am I looking for? Something like morning light, I tell myself. The lantern glow of untouched skin. My lost girlhood, perhaps. But it is all untrue, Noora: I am looking for you.

Some time ago, the girl in the room next to my own took a liking to me. Her name was Leela. She knocked on my door one late evening a few months ago, well after most of the hostel had gone to sleep. The knock startled me; no one had knocked on my door for months and I wondered whether someone had unintentionally banged against the door as they passed. But then I heard the knock again, this time more insistent.

I rose slowly. I was not yet asleep. In fact, I was quite busy. I'd gotten into the habit—every night, even now, even if the electricity has gone out and I have to do it by candlelight—of counting lentils. I keep them in a plastic tin, these lentils. Most of them are either yellow toor dal lentils or dark brown channa lentils, but my favorites are the rare pink and orange masoor dal lentils. So smooth and delicate, almost wisps—nothing like the fat and coarse channa—and their color, Noora! Like a sunrise. Like the hidden, singing insides of seashells. Like your fingertips.

Most nights I count them and put them back in the tin. On other nights, when I'm not feeling well, I place them in little piles, separated by color, and watch as each of these piles grows and grows. It's mysterious to me, and awfully troubling, when the number changes from one night to the next. I think, Someone is stealing them! Even if there are *more* lentils than in my last count I feel strangely betrayed. As if they are conniving to split apart, to haunt me, to be unruly, like children. No, there must be exactly nine hundred and eighty-six. Four hundred and eleven toor. Three hundred and seventy-eight channa. And one hundred ninety-seven of my beloved masoor.

I was almost done counting the masoor—at one hundred and fifty-four—when I heard the second knock. I opened the door and made out Leela's face in the dark hallway, wrapped in a woolen shawl. We'd passed many times in the mess hall but had rarely spoken. She was smiling.

"What is it, beti? Can't you sleep?"

"No, it's not that, auntie," she said, her voice bright against the shadowed hallway. "I was making tea on my hot plate but I've run out of sugar." She stepped inside my room with a bold stride. It was then that it struck me: the daring of these girls. They were all—each one—just like the girl who'd stolen my ribbon. Weaving through the streets, laughing, the ribbon fluttering like a sail behind them. Unafraid of the seas into which they sailed. Leela eyed the room. Her gaze passed over my hemp rope bed, my tiny suitcase provided by the Indian government, and the pile of lentils on the floor. "Why, auntie." She laughed. "What a strange time to make dal."

I only smiled. She left with the sugar and came back a few minutes later with two cups of tea. Then she sat cross-legged on my bed, as if we'd known each other for years, and said, "So tell me, auntie, how did you come to be here."

I smiled again.

I was with him—somewhere in Pakistan—for almost two years. I sat in that darkened hut, watching the pattern of the sunlight as it slithered from one end of the room to the other, and waited. In the beginning I was sure someone would come for me. That they would find me locked up in that hut and take me away from him. But no one came. The days crept by: he'd force himself on me every night, he'd sleep, I'd lie awake, he'd go away in the morning, I'd watch the light seep from the room, he'd return in the evening with four roti he'd bought for my dinner and my next day's breakfast, and then he'd take me again. My days were quiet. I'd stopped crying after the first month or two. The dark of the hut, with its frail shafts of light, became more familiar to me than even my parents' faces. How could it not: every night he killed them again.

He told me, when he first brought me here, that no one would ever come for me. He'd say, with great confidence, "You're probably assumed dead. All the Hindu girls in your village are, you know." Then he'd padlock the door, force himself on me, and say, "You're lucky I found you." I don't recall, for the first few months—as we traveled over rutted roads and arrived finally at this hut—having ever really looked at him. But then his pockmarked face began to slowly form itself in my mind; his breath on my neck was sometimes sweet and heavy with hashish, sometimes rancid with tobacco and rotten meat. His eyes were dark, with heavy eyelids and thick eyebrows, the whites of them clear in the mornings but smoky and yellowed in the evenings. He had a thin, struggling beard—perhaps from his face being scarred—and once, when he came home, a bit of food was stuck in the hairs. It startled me—in a way that nothing has startled me since—that I reached out and plucked it from his beard. It seemed to startle him too. It'd been many weeks since he'd brought me to the hut and the tenderness of the act, the utter decency of it, was like a sudden spell of rain: I no longer knew whether I belonged inside or outside that hut.

A month later I was pregnant.

On the night I went into labor the pain was so intense that I woke him in the middle of the night and asked him calmly to get some help. He looked at me suspiciously but then I must've paled because he returned a few minutes later with an old, wizened woman. She was bent with age, and half blind because she kept screaming for light. "How do you expect me to deliver this baby with this useless little wick?" she grumbled, pointing at the one candle he placed beside her.

"You couldn't see if the sun dropped out of your wrinkled old *choot*," he said.

She seemed not to hear him. "Light, more light," she shrieked again. "And more water."

The pain continued until early morning. I was delirious with it. The pallet on which I lay was awash in blood. And the old lady was foul-tempered. She'd wipe down my brow and scuttle away to check the bleeding then emerge again to complain about being woken up in the middle of the night. "When I was young we didn't wake the others just for *this*," she'd hiss, her gnarled, leathery hands coming up like tree bark. When I whimpered with pain she peered into my face and laughed. "It'll die, anyway," she said. "I had seven myself. Only three lived. All that trouble for nothing." Toward dawn there was a series of large contractions. The old woman bent low and whispered again but the pain blurred her voice. Only her breath reached me, moist and smelling of horse manure and wide, green meadows. I nearly fainted from the pain when, from a great distance, I heard a tiny cry. Yours.

The old woman wrapped you in a blanket and rested you on my chest. "Your Noora is healthy."

"Noora?" I asked.

"That's her name."

"Noora, Noora," I repeated. I liked the sound, but I'd never heard that name before. "What does it mean?" I asked.

She smiled for the first time and it was then that I realized she only had three teeth in her mouth. All that time with her—as she held my hand and bent over my face—and I'd just noticed. "Noora," she said, still smiling though the smile didn't reach her eyes, "means light."

She turned and opened the door and it was the first time, since I'd been in the hut, that it was unlocked. She swung it wide and something like apology swept over her face. "One of them only lived for a day. A girl." She paused and I thought she might sigh but she didn't; she wasn't a woman who sighed. "Smart too," she said. "She knew a day of this was more than enough."

Though I ache to remember details about them now, I tried, in those first few months after you were born, not to think of your grandparents. What was there to think about? They burned like everything else. He found me sitting on the stoop of our ruined house. I don't know what I must've looked like but he said I was so covered in soot and ash that if I hadn't blinked, he wouldn't have known I was there.

And so that is how I think of you, Noora: born in the blink of an eye.

He ignored you, mostly, in those first few weeks. I was grateful for that. The hut filled with the warm, fecund scent of old milk and damp wool and he hardly seemed to notice. Only once, when I was feeding you, did he look over and say, "They're mine, not hers."

You were six weeks old when the soldier knocked on the door. It was locked, of course. I huddled with you in the corner, hardly breathing. But then a youthful voice called out, "Hello, hello. Anybody there?" There was a pause, some shuffling. I gripped my hand over your mouth to keep you from crying. "No need to be afraid, madam," the voice continued, growing firmer, more assured. "My name is Gopal Das. I'm from the Indian Army." I eyed the window then the door. What if *he'd* sent goondas just to beat me, or to take you? I placed you in the cradle I'd fashioned out of old blankets and a bit of straw. Then I rose and tiptoed quietly to the slit in the window. He was very young, hardly older than me. But he was wearing a military uniform with red badges across his chest. "Open the window, madam," he said. "You're safe with me."

I should've never opened it because you see, Noora, he said *I* was safe. He never said a thing about you.

I eventually opened the window and indicated we were inside; he was delighted to see me—as if I were his long-lost sister—and he grew breathless as he told me to wait, to not make a noise, and that he'd be back with his senior officer in no time at all. He practically skipped away from the hut, his baton raised, and returned an hour later with an officer with even more red badges on his uniform and a middle-aged woman in a white sari and glasses, with a large black mole on her chin as round as her face. "Here she is," the young soldier proclaimed, beaming like a child. We were all gathered again around the window.

The middle-aged woman saw you in my arms and her expression soured. She glanced at the senior officer. He said nothing.

"The father," she began, pointing toward you. "Is he Muslim?"

I nodded. I held you closer. I wanted to tell them everything, all at once—how your grandfather had herded us into one of the bedrooms and locked the door, how the mob had torched our house, smoke and then flames seeping under the cracks and through the walls, how I'd snaked out of the window, too small to fit your grandparents, and how your grandmother, just before my head disappeared through the window, had taken my face in her tear-streaked hands and said, "You are my heart." And how one of the mob, as he passed the gate, had gotten his shirt caught on a spoke. He saw me when he stopped to loosen it. I wanted to tell them that that was how I came to be here, with you, because of something as simple and as heartbreaking as a piece of cloth caught on an iron gate—but the words wouldn't come.

"The child," the woman said. "She cannot come."

"Where?"

"Back to India, of course." Her voice was slow and measured, and yet I struggled to understand.

"But why? She's my daughter."

"But she's a citizen of Pakistan. She's a Muslim."

I glared at the two soldiers. They were looking at the ground. Then I looked at her. How could she say such a thing? A woman, and a Hindu? Her mole grew blacker and I stared at it and stared at it and then I spit at it. The woman jumped back. "Then I won't come," I said.

There was a silence. A crow flew overhead and I heard its cawing. The older soldier finally spoke. He took a step toward me. His voice was low and deep like the night sky. "You must, beti. Now that we have found you, you must return to India."

"I won't," I said. "Not without my Noora." By then you'd begun to whimper, as if you knew what was to come.

The woman scowled. She pushed up her glasses: she cupped the edge of the right lens and lifted them gingerly off the bridge of her nose then tucked them, with great care, higher on her face. If you can hold those with such tenderness, I wanted to say, imagine how I hold my Noora. "You have no choice," she said. "There are governmental treaties we must follow."

"What treaties? What governments?"

"Between India and Pakistan."

"But this is *my child*."

"She's a child of Pakistan," the old soldier said solemnly. "And you, my dear, are not."

They left, telling me they'd be back in two days. I couldn't decide what to do. I thought of running away with you when they came for me and knocked down the door, but what then? I hardly even knew where I was. How could I make a living for us? Besides, what if he found us? Then I considered staying. I remembered that feeling of sudden rain; maybe I could remain in the hut and continue on as I had for the past two years. I thought about the days since I'd arrived there, and the long hours of watching thin columns of sunlight stride across the room like armies, and the lonely nights of waiting for him to be done, to sleep, so I could lie awake, listening to his snoring, and think of your grandmother's paneer, to be like that pebble skipping across time. But then you came, and everything took on a brilliance, a meaning, so that even when he smothered me, tugged at my hair in his throes, slammed his body against mine, I listened. I listened for you. I listened for your breathing. For you were alive, you see. And I, Noora, after that first time, was dead.

I had to keep you; I decided we would stay.

But remember what I told you: suffering is strange. That very night he came home and threw the four roti on the ground. "Did anybody come here?" he growled. "Tell me. Tell me the truth."

I held my hand steady as I reached for the roti. "No, no one."

He eyed me; his gaze followed me around the room. He lit a cigarette. "There's talk that Indian soldiers have been snooping around here. Knocking on doors." He reached over and grabbed my arm. "You remember what to do if they come around, don't you?"

"I remember."

"What?"

"Tell them you're my brother. And that our parents died in the riots."

"Good girl." He squeezed my arm tighter. "And make sure they don't see *her.*" He blew out a band of smoke, his yellowed eyes burrowing into my own, and then he took the cigarette from his mouth and pushed the lit end into my arm. The sizzle reached me before the pain. He smiled. "Just so you don't forget," he said.

The next morning I woke on the edge of a peculiar dream. I was at a river crossing. I could see clear to the other side. There was even a boat, as if that would make things easier. Oars too. But something kept insisting, insisting, and the throb of insistence was like the river. I woke up and looked down at my arm. Such a tiny crater. Perfect and round and raw where he'd put out his cigarette. Raw in the way that cinnamon is raw. The sizzle when the tip of his cigarette had touched my skin was simply papad in hot oil, just like that: common and unconfusing. *Wound* seemed too magnificent a word for it.

I looked at you, asleep in your makeshift cradle.

In the end it was the burn of the cigarette, really. Even when I ignored it, went about the morning as if nothing had happened, it kept throbbing and throbbing until I peered down at it—as if it were a raucous child in the quiet of a twilit temple—and said, Shh.

But it wouldn't hush. Not for a minute.

Here's what it told me: that he would hurt you as he'd hurt me. And though a cigarette burn can't talk it *can* say this: it is easier to look at death than at pain. In one the grief lingers and then passes with time. In the other, it is relentless. It is unerring. And it throbs—said the burn—like me.

Funny, isn't it?

And so I looked at you and I looked at you and I held you and I held you and then I killed you. I killed you.

Leela has been gone for some time now. Married and moved to Pune. I never told her any of this. Why? This is not a story for the young. But on one of our last nights sharing tea, a few days before she was to be married, she sat cross-legged on my bed, as she always did, and teased me about the piles of lentils. "Come now, auntie, you must tell me, why *do* you count those lentils, night after night?"

I thought at first that I would only smile, like I always did when she asked me that question. But then I thought of that ribbon. Lost so many years now. I could still see it twirling in the wind. What happened to that girl? The one who stood in the silence of a summer afternoon and felt her heart beating. Where is that girl? That heart?

"They're so tiny. There must be *thousands*. Look, even your hands are shaking." Leela took my wrists and turned them over. And there was that cigarette burn, throbbing. Throbbing. All through these many years.

"You must tell me," she persisted.

"Because," I finally said, "it distracts me."

"From what?" she said. "Besides, there's television for that. You could even buy a radio."

"None of those are loud enough."

"For what?" She laughed.

I looked at the piles of lentils. It takes me exactly thirty minutes to count out nine hundred and eighty-six lentils. That is what I give myself every day: thirty minutes. "The sound," I said, "of throbbing."

It's raining tonight. The candle is burning out. The piles are nearly complete but my eyes grow heavy. I'm slower today, more tired. But just as I'm nearly finished the candle goes out. And I think, If only I could've had a few more moments of light.

THE OPPOSITE OF SEX

Mohan was dispatched to a tiny village—ten miles south of the nearest town of English Bazar—to map the new border between India and East Pakistan. His job, as the youngest member of the Calcutta Chapter of the Indian Geographical Society, was to survey the region that had just been bisected, and submit the findings so that the details of the border could be finalized. It was a serious task matched—surpassed, really—only by his own seriousness. He'd been orphaned at the age of five. A maternal uncle, who was a confirmed Brahmachari, had raised him. When he was six, Mohan had asked his uncle to buy him small painted figurines of a man and woman, dressed in colorful Rajasthani costume, holding a tiny baby in their arms. A goat and cow stood on either side. Mohan's parents weren't farmers but the toys reminded him of them. But his uncle hardly even glanced at them; instead he looked down at Mohan, and said, "What are you? A girl?" Then even his uncle died, and Mohan left his legal studies, which his uncle had insisted upon, and began to study cartography. He didn't quite understand why. He only understood that he wanted to study something with one side to it. The law had two. But cartography had one: lines could be disputed, armies could fight, people could die, but really, when it came right down to it, maps could tell a truth that men could not.

It was immediately after Mohan's mapping of this new border that his troubles began. Three troubles to be exact.

The first was that Lalita's father committed suicide. He hung himself. Upon hearing this, Mohan didn't feel particularly bad. He barely knew the man, after all. But Lalita. Now Lalita was a different matter.

The first time he'd seen her was one morning when she was with a group of young women gathered near the village well, chattering and laughing and teasing. It was one of those wells that did not rise above the level of the ground; this he observed with interest. Wooden planks covered the opening, and one merely had to lift the hinged door cut into the planks and drop in a bucket. Eventually, his gaze left the brown planks and traveled to the brightly dressed women. He looked at each of them in turn, and with a certain degree of surprise. He had not in many years seen a group of people so unabashedly happy. It was as if happiness in his life, even the witnessing of it, had taken to the shadows. One that he knew lived somewhere—maybe in tunnels dug deep beneath the streets on which he walked, or growing like a mold behind the walls of his flat—but it had not shown itself. Not to him. Not for a very long time.

How long ago? he wondered once. How long *had* it been since he'd been truly happy? The memory that rose within him was so frightening that he pushed it back down instantly. The memory, of course, was of when he was five years old, just before his parents had died. His father's friend had come for a visit. He'd stayed for three nights, and on the second night, he'd snuck into Mohan's room. He'd crept in on the third night as well. Both nights, he'd left only after making Mohan promise not to say a word to anyone. "Especially not to your parents," he'd said. "If you speak of this, if you *do* anything, something awful will happen." But Mohan's mother, a week later, finding him sitting alone and staring silently at a wall, had coaxed it out of him. He'd told her a little, not much. But even so, three months later, his parents had been hit by an oncoming lorry and had died.

And so, at the age of five, and every day since then, Mohan decided—against all reason and against all time—that he was the one who'd killed them.

Mohan looked again at the well. He studied Lalita particularly. He saw that she, of all the young women, seemed happiest. How was that possible? She was certainly not the prettiest: her nose was too wide and her skin much too dark, and he squinted and saw that she had a large birthmark splattered across her chin and left cheek. From where Mohan was standing, it looked like someone had taken mud and smeared it over her face. And yet. And yet she was happy. He couldn't understand it. He forced himself to turn away from her. By this time the young women at the well—six in all—began to disperse with their pots of water. They were moving quickly toward a turn in the road, balancing the water pots on their hips. Now he could only see their backsides. So full and round and alive that he nearly cried. Just as they turned the corner Lalita looked over her shoulder and said something to one of her friends. The two smiled, shimmering together with that same happiness Mohan had noticed before. But then Lalita did something odd. Well, not odd, but beautiful. She shifted the clay pot of water from her right hip to her left. She pushed it up against the curve of her waist, wrapped her arm around the neck of the pot, and disappeared around the bend. Mohan knelt to the ground; he could taste the earthen dampness clinging to her waist. He knew then that he'd been wrong: she wasn't simply *happy*; happiness could not possibly explain the strange loveliness, the utter seductiveness, of that gesture. No, what Lalita had was something even more audacious than happiness. What was it? Mohan trembled. He tried not to flee: he fussed with the transit; he checked the level of the tripod; he practically ran after her.

Sitting on his bed that afternoon, after lunch, Mohan decided that the clay of the pot and the bronze of Lalita's skin were the only true substances. They were why the rains fell, why the sun rose. His fingers had traced them all his life. Then he knew. He knew what Lalita had that the others didn't, that *he* didn't: she had sex. In fact, he realized, what she had was the opposite of what he had. But what was it that he had? What was the opposite of sex? It seemed like a question without an answer. Like, where does reality stop and unreality begin? Or, what goes deeper, the human soul or the human imagination? But this one had an answer. *That* much Mohan knew. He knew that the opposite of sex was fear. And fear was something he had an abundance of. He turned and looked at the wall: blue, watermarks sweeping down its length like curtains. It suddenly felt as if this was all he'd ever done: sit and stare at walls. With this thought his back straightened, his mouth grew resolute. And he knew what he had to do.

He leapt up, ran out of the door, and within a week learned everything there was to know about Lalita. She had failed her tenth class exams and was now at home, taking care of her father. Her mother had died just a few years ago, when Lalita had been fourteen. Her father, a wealthy local landowner, had kept his daughter close but had sent his son to be educated in Durgapur. The old man was tough, shrewd, but he doted on his daughter, the villagers said. Gave her far too many liberties. For instance, with a house full of servants, and the girl of marriageable age, why allow her to fetch water, why even let her out of the house? Why, indeed? Mohan smiled. The villagers looked at him curiously. Why do you want to know? they asked. It's important for my surveying work to understand the community, Mohan said. The villagers—all farmers, none of whom had gone past fifth class—nodded gravely. The nugget in all of this was that Lalita's father was looking for matches. Someone local, so his daughter would be close, and someone with a head for the farming business. Mohan had neither of these qualities but that scarcely deterred him. He could move; there was nothing in Calcutta that held him. And the farming business could hardly be more complicated than triangulation and theodolites and all those illusory meridians.

He decided the next day to go and visit Lalita's father. Maybe even ask for her hand on the spot. That was what courageous people did, and that's what he would do. He planned out what he would say, and how he would say it: be firm, insistent, yet mildly polite, he told himself, practicing in the mirror the night before the visit. Be heroic. But Mohan never got the chance. And what was more, the visit with Lalita's father, he decided afterward, was when everything started going terribly wrong. Not the visit itself—that went fine—but what sent everything veering uncontrollably from the dream of Lalita into the realm of nightmare was Mohan's grotesque underestimation of something that should have been obvious. Should've been crystalline, most certainly to a cartographer: Mohan had underestimated the power of land. Lalita's father, though he was crippled, had practically seethed with it.

The room he was shown into was large and opulent. It smelled of sandalwood. There were silk divans and pillars of carved teakwood and a floor of polished marble. Toward one end was a sort of dais, on which the old man, his legs useless from a polio infection, was seated. Mohan was instructed to sit opposite him and a servant brought out a tray loaded with tea and colorful sweets and three kinds of savory mixture. The old man, once Mohan was seated, looked at him with delight and said, "So you want to marry my daughter."

How had he known?

The old man didn't wait for a response. He said, "What do you see when you look at her?"

"How do you mean?" Mohan said.

"You *have* looked at her, haven't you?" Her father smiled.

"Well, yes."

"Then what is it you see?" he said.

Mohan thought of Lalita, the earthen pot nestled in the curve of her hip, her wide nose, the birthmark on her face swaying before him like a strange and erotic pendulum. He looked at her father and told himself, Be heroic. "I see my future wife," he said.

The old man didn't even seem to hear him. "Do you know what I see?" he asked.

The room was silent. The servant who had brought the tea things reappeared and waited just beyond a silk curtain at the edge of the room. "I see dirt. Not just any dirt, Mr. Mohan, rich, black dirt. The kind where a mere whisper will sprout a seed. The kind that's fed by every river there is, the Mahananda, the Yamuna, Ganga, the Nile! You see what I'm saying? The kind of dirt men were meant to plow. Do you see?"

"Yes," Mohan said. And that was the end. Moments later the old man signaled for the servant, who showed Mohan to the door. He stumbled into the evening light and spun in circles, knowing, incontrovertibly and without a clue as to why, that he had failed.

Two weeks after his visit with Lalita's father Mohan heard from one of the villagers that she was engaged to be married. Her betrothed was a young man from a neighboring village, with land of his own. The dowry—one thousand acres, to be transferred on the day of the wedding—would increase the groom's landholdings tenfold. This news—the solidity of it, as if her engagement was a thick metal vault he now had to find a way to open—caught Mohan unawares. He sat at his desk and brooded. Only his old servant and companion, Basu, looked in on him and commiserated. "A girl of such wealth." He breathed. "And those hips, those moist aams—"

"Shut up," Mohan said.

"And as sweet as a rossogolla," Basu added. Mohan glared at him.

"Use your head," Basu said.

Mohan looked up.

"You don't have any land, obviously, all you have is your head. Use it." Then he left out of the back kitchen door after preparing Mohan's dinner.

As night fell Mohan stared at his now cold plate of rice and goat curry. The chunks of goat had congealed in the gravy and looked like trapped canoes in a muddy river. The moonlight streaming through the window added an extra element of the sinister. This is the end, he thought. My

Lalita is lost. He looked at the piles and piles of maps, papers, and figures at the edge of his desk and thought: my head. What's the use: there's nothing in my head. It's all in my heart. He gaped some more at the maps, his surveying work stacked up, waiting to be used to finalize the border between West Bengal and East Pakistan. The turn of the Mahananda near English Bazar, the flow of the river south through the village in which he was stationed, and then, still farther south, the lands owned by Lalita's father.

Mohan pushed the plate of food aside. He brought the sketches closer. Most of them were merely projections. The contours of the land, the river, and the general topography were all basically already bisected. All Mohan was sent here to do was to map it, and then to make recommendations as to slight variations, if necessary. *If necessary*, he repeated to himself. He looked at the map of Lalita's father's land; it ran right along the border, with both the village and the land in India. But what if his land ended up in East Pakistan, and his house remained in India? Out of necessity? The projection could be easily doctored, and then Lalita's father would lose the one thing that bound his daughter's engagement: the dowry of a thousand acres. He would have enough to live on, about twenty acres or so, but the rest would disappear. Then Mohan—the landless intellectual, the compassionate savior—could step in and volunteer, out of the goodness of his heart, to marry his daughter, the shamed, impoverished victim of a broken engagement. It was brilliant. It was using his head.

Mohan submitted the doctored maps; it took less than a month for them to be released. And it was then—the very next day—that Lalita's father committed suicide. When Basu told him, the first thing Mohan wondered was how a man without the use of his legs could hang himself. Had the servant lifted him to the noose, or had the noose been low enough for a seated man? As to that, how had he constructed the noose in the first place? How could he possibly have tied it to a high enough place, or even a low place that was high enough for a man to hang?

"Did he leave a note?" Mohan asked.

"It said he couldn't live anymore. Not as a landless man."

"But he still had twenty acres!"

Basu looked at him with suspicion. "How do you know?"

"Because I've surveyed every inch of it, you moorkh." Basu still eyed him warily. "How is Lalita?"

"She's in mourning."

"And the engagement?"

"Off."

Mohan smiled, despite himself. He knew what he would kiss first: her birthmark.

It was, of course, unfortunate that the old man had to die but otherwise things were going exactly as he had planned. He had only to be patient, and wait. But once the period of mourning was over, his second trouble set in: Basu nearly skipped through the door with this latest gossip: the groom-to-be, the one who had been promised the thousand acres as a dowry, had offered to marry Lalita without it.

"*What?*" Mohan started.

"What selflessness," Basu said, taking on a somber tone. "Gandhiji would be proud."

Mohan rolled his eyes. What a bastard. He would marry her anyway. What a show-off. What was he supposed to do now?

There was no need for him to have contemplated action because the answer, in the form of further gossip from Basu, reached him a few days later. "Now," he said, "she's refusing to marry *him*."

Mohan stared at him. "How is that possible?"

"She's called it off. Again."

A jolt of hope passed through Mohan. "Has she said, I mean, have you heard who she wants to marry instead?"

"Apparently," Basu said, "nobody."

"But how? How will she live?"

"Maybe off the twenty acres you seem to know so much about," he said, smiling.

This was too much. Mohan set off, practically running from his cottage toward Lalita's house. He passed the well with its flat wooden lid, ripped right through the center of the village with its one sundries shop and post office cum teahouse, and didn't even bother to offer a prayer at the tiny Durga temple at the edge of the fields. The villagers looked on in amazement. They had never seen their timid surveyor in such a state.

Lalita opened the door. She was even more intoxicating than in his memory. The birthmark on her face was a gathering gloom. A typhoon. A pier. It was shark-infested waters. It was all he had ever wanted. "Where are your servants?" he asked.

"I can't afford to keep them," she said. Then she said, "Who are you?"

Mohan sighed. "I knew your father." She looked at him for a moment before letting him inside. The house had taken on a sad, tragic air. The dais where he'd sat with her father looked forlorn, empty, as if it were a ruined schoolhouse where children had once played. Even Lalita's face had darkened since he'd last seen her, or no, he thought, not darkened, but grown older. He felt—in this moment—the first pangs of conscience, and guilt. Maybe he should not have divided the land, maybe he should have kept it intact, and let her marry that young man. Maybe he should have let them be young together.

"See here," he said, "why don't you marry? Your father would've wanted—"

"How do you know?" she said.

"I told you, I knew him."

She studied him. "Aren't you that man? The one walking around with all that equipment, snooping around the village."

"Well, yes," Mohan said.

They stood silently, not exactly facing each other, but more facing the dais, as if her father was still there.

"Like I was saying, you should marry."

"Who?"

Mohan thought then of the boy he'd been. And of how, at the age of five, that boy had left him. He said, "Why not the young man you were engaged to?"

"Because without the dowry, I don't know whether he's marrying me out of love or pity."

"*With* the dowry, you wouldn't have known whether it was for love or money."

"Neither is as bad as pity," she said.

Mohan looked at her. It came to him that he was in the presence of something he could not possibly understand. She was a minefield, and there he stood, unable to move. Her nose, her birthmark like the spill of blood, the memory of her damp hips, they were the waiting sorrows, no matter which way he turned. Mohan closed his eyes and thought of a map. Any map. All those lines, hiding all those lives: strung between us like hissing electric wire.

A few weeks after his meeting with Lalita is when his third and final trouble set in. A Muslim family, subsistence farmers living outside the village, had been killed. Father, mother, all four children, murdered. When Mohan heard the news he didn't have to ask, he knew: they were killed by a Hindu mob. Since the details of the border had been released—*his* details of the border—the village had undergone a transformation. It was no longer a quiet farming village; it was now an angry village. The Hindus were angry that their land (though truthfully, most of it had belonged to Lalita's father) had gone to East Pakistan, to the Muslims. They first looted the sundries shop, which belonged to a Muslim, and not satisfied with that, they resorted to slaughter.

Mohan was terrified. He was not Muslim, true, but he had been the one responsible for the *necessary* changes. Everyone in the village knew exactly who'd drawn the last line. He was afraid to go outside. He sent Basu to the post office one afternoon and he returned with a telegram from Mohan's boss, D6. His name was actually Mr. Debnath, but Mohan had always thought of him as D6. The telegram said he would arrive in a week's time for a "progress review," but Mohan, squatting in his darkened room—he no longer lit the lantern in the evenings—knew the real reason.

He met D6 at the station in English Bazar. When he emerged from the train he was thinner than Mohan remembered. He was wearing a light blue shirt that showed rings of sweat stains under his arms, and though his shock of white hair was tousled from the train journey, his mustache was neatly combed. He did not smile when he spotted Mohan. And when he raised his hand to shake Mohan's, his sixth finger, the extra one D6 had been born with next to his pinky finger, pointed straight at Mohan like the barrel of a small gun.

By the time they returned to the village it was dinnertime. Basu had prepared a special meal of rice pulao, deep fried capsicum with chicken, and machher jhol. They both ate slowly, disinterestedly. Midway through the meal D6 looked at Mohan. "Why did you move the border?" he asked. Of course Mohan was prepared for this question. But in that moment his mind went blank, and he sat and thought about each of the words separately, as if they were the shattered pieces of a vase or a plate that he was trying to fit back together. "I don't recall, sir," he finally said. D6 stared at him, and went back to mixing his chicken curry and rice. Since it had no joints, and so could not be bent, D6's sixth finger struck against the steel plate like the light tapping of a spoon. Mohan had never eaten with D6 before; he was fascinated by it. It had a certain rhythm: the tap, tap, tapping of mixing the rice, putting it in his mouth, gathering another bite. He had always respected D6 and D6 seemed to like him well enough, but he was a quiet man, and Mohan was never really sure what he was thinking. But the finger: the finger never tired of speaking to him.

The following day when Mohan woke up, D6 was already at the table, deep in study, maps and sketches spread across the table. The village was quiet. Unnaturally so, Mohan thought.

"We're going to the border," D6 announced. They hired the same car as the previous day and drove a few miles in the direction of the border. The countryside in late September was dry and brown after the long summer. The Mahananda was as thin as a stream. It was still early, the sun barely over the horizon and rising slowly, like bread. A few hundred yards short of the border D6 asked the driver to stop alongside an open field. Mohan recognized the place though neither spoke as they trudged to the top of a low promontory. It faced east, and Mohan looked out across the fields and in that open air, that cool morning, he felt none of the guilt or dread or anxiety of the past few weeks. He felt only the Brahmaputra in front of him, and the Ganga behind him, and knew that somewhere in East Pakistan they met, well away from English Bazar and the thousand measly acres that had caused such madness. They emptied like lovers into the Bay of Bengal. He could almost hear the meeting of these two mighty rivers, the surge after surge of pure cold Himalayan runoff.

"Do you know why Manthara was the most evil of all, even more than Ravana?" D6 asked.

Manthara? Mohan had no idea who D6 was talking about. The only clue was Ravana. His thoughts raced. He strained to remember everything he could about the *Ramayana*: the story of Rama and Sita and the forest and Hanuman carrying the mountain was easy to recall, but Manthara? Who was she? His mind spun like a wheel and came up with nothing.

D6 was looking east again, deep into the fields. After a long silence he said, "She was Kaikeyi's servant, Mr. Mohan, the one who was aware that the queen had been promised two boons from the king. She was the one who convinced Kaikeyi to call them in: one was to place Bharata, her own son, on the throne rather than Rama, and the other was to banish Rama for fourteen years to the forest. The king, you see, had no choice, he had to abide by his promise." He turned to Mohan. His blue-white hair whipped in the wind and against the dark brown of his skin looked like the meeting of earth and sky. "Do you see, Mr. Mohan?"

"No, sir, I don't."

"She was a nobody. A servant. A humpbacked old crone. And yet she changed the course of a kingdom. Of the gods. If that is possible then we are powerless, aren't we, against the slightest little tick in our beds."

Mohan looked at the ground. He raised his eyes just far enough to spy the sixth finger hanging from D6's right hand. The useless little finger that had perhaps determined D6's destiny, he thought. He wondered what it would be like to touch it, to snap it off his hand like a twig.

"The Government of India may try you for treason, Mr. Mohan," D6 said, turning to walk down to the car.

A shot of ice water ran up Mohan's spine. Blood pooled in his feet. "Treason?"

"Maybe you should be tried for murder instead," D6 said placidly. "But human life has always been worth less than land, hasn't it?"

Mohan had trouble raising his legs. He stumbled on a branch and kept walking, blindly. Then he started running after D6, who was taking long purposeful strides, though Mohan's were as formless and as jerky as a child's. "But, Mr. Debnath," he called after him.

They were back at the car by the time D6 looked at Mohan. He smiled, a wistful look on his face. "Do you see that mist over there, Mr. Mohan," he said. Mohan turned to look. In the distance, hovering over the fields, was a thin strip of gray mist, not yet touched by the sun, so still lingering, still low and lovely. He had not noticed it before. He hardly noticed it now. "Isn't it the saddest thing?" D6 said. "To be made of nothing? To know you'll just burn away in the end?"

Mohan stood, looking at the mist.

The driver emerged from a clump of trees where he'd been dozing and opened each of their doors. They didn't go to the border, as Mohan had expected, but turned back toward the village. The drive back felt far longer than the drive there. Mohan sat slumped in his seat, an expression of both shock and despair on his face. By the time they got to the village he was thinking of Lalita, of the first time he had seen her and how her arm had wrapped like an embrace around the clay earthen pot.

How long ago it seemed.

When they reached his cottage they entered through the back of the house, by way of the kitchen, and it was only then that Mohan noticed the people who had gathered outside his front door, peering in through his window. He jumped back in surprise. He stopped D6, who was still in the kitchen, and slammed the door shut.

"What? What is it?" D6 asked.

Mohan was shaking violently. He clenched his fists. "A mob," he said. "Outside." Sounds of shouting and banging on the front door reached them. When he opened the back door a crack, to see if the car was still there, Mohan saw that one or two of the men were making their way toward the back, and the driver had gone running. He slammed the door shut. The kitchen had a barred window in the back and through this the two men began throwing rocks. They yelled to the men in the front, They're back here! Mohan and D6 were now pressed against the door to the front room, away from the rocks that were being flung at them. It was early afternoon and the sun glinted off the raised machetes of the men gathered now in the back. Some of the men had sticks. Mohan counted a dozen, maybe more. The rocks kept coming, and they were saved only by the fact that the barred window kept out most of the bigger ones. Mohan shielded his face, already cut and bleeding, and when he peeked through his fingers he saw the rage in the faces of the men. You're a traitor, they yelled. You gave our land to the katwas, they yelled. They were crowded at the window, white teeth glinting like the machetes and the dark, dark darkness of their skin crowding out the light. Mohan thought of the front door but he knew, *he knew* that the latch door on the well was open and that if he and D6 made a run for it, they would chase them into the well.

He looked at D6. He too was shielding his face. His sixth finger stuck out of the side of his face and Mohan thought that this was what he had always wanted. A limb or an appendage or an organ that was unbendable, unyielding, attached to his body but free of it.

The mob pushed closer. The door rattled on its hinges.

Mohan had never believed that people's lives flashed before their eyes in the moments before death, but in a way, his did: he saw his father's friend. His heart recoiled. The men with the machetes disappeared because they, in the end, were no kind of threat. But this man—his father's friend— *he* was indiscriminate. Mohan pushed tighter against the kitchen wall, felt the roughness of the sheet his face was being thrust into. No, he didn't care. He didn't care if you were his friend's son, or a dreaming little boy, or a boy breathing slowly, sleeping under a thin summer sheet: he took a machete to them all.

SUCH A MIGHTY RIVER

Alok Debnath sucked on his sixth finger, dangling off the pinky of his right hand, for eighty-four years before he lost it. It was so simple: one quick slash of the knife and there it lay. On the table. Detached. It was moist and trembling, like a snail without its shell, and he looked at it with curiosity, as if it were a museum piece or an artifact that had once belonged to someone else. But it was his, all right. This recognition lasted only a moment because in the next, blood began to pour out of the raw flesh and exposed bone where the finger had once been. Even the little snail on the table was now floating in a pool of blood. Alok Debnath clutched his left hand over the gushing wound. Blood seeped through his fingers and landed on the dirt floor with the pretty plop of fat raindrops. All the blood in his body seemed to be emptying itself through its new faucet. He screamed and screamed. "Shut up, shut up, *shut up*," Naagi said. Someone came up behind him and stuffed a rag into his mouth. With his mouth plugged up Alok Debnath's eyes watered, darted around the room. Everyone—Naagi, the fat man, the little bird—eyed him nervously. Except for Rekha. Rekha just stood there placidly, voluptuously, watching him. Who was this woman? Had he loved her once? He might have— he couldn't be sure, his mind was muddy—but he was certain he did not love her now.

It was toward the end of December, a little after the ayananta but before the children's winter holidays, when Rekha didn't come. He had bought her for the afternoon but she failed to show. Alok Debnath waited nervously. It was unlike her to be late; he was without doubt, in the case of Rekha, of certain things: she would brutalize him with her cruelty, seduce him with her ass, and she was always, always on time. It was nearing five o'clock; his daughter would return at six with the children, his son-in-law at eight. Alok Debnath waited by the window. The street his daughter lived on looked out onto a row of affluent houses in Taktakpur. Her husband had made money in textiles, and theirs was one of the biggest homes on the block. But Alok Debnath cared for none of it: the big house, the money, much less his avaricious son-in-law. He sat morosely at the window of his lavish room sucking on his sixth finger and wondered what to do. He shuffled around the room, unsure what he was looking for, then he put on his coat and his scarf and his knitted hat and walked out of the door without a paisa to his name. He even forgot his keys. When he got to the end of the block he remembered: he was looking for Rekha. With this thought his mind and his spirits lifted like a kite in a strong wind, and Alok Debnath breathed deeply of the chill winter air. The scent of woodsmoke and the Ganga mingled and entered his blood, swelled his heart, and he set off again with conviction. After he'd walked about ten paces he found it was no use, his mind was dull again, but he continued doggedly. It would come to him. And it did, four blocks later: don't worry, he said aloud and with great solemnity, "I'm coming, Sarojini, I'm coming for you."

Alok Debnath had just turned eighty-four. It was the winter of 1976 and he was living with his married daughter in Benares. His daughter had three children but he preferred not to see them. They were noisy, they confused him, and they pulled on his sixth finger as if it was one of their plastic toys. The youngest, three-year-old Bunny, once grabbed it as she would a handful of bhelpuri and said, "Why is it all wrinkly, nanaji?"

"Because it's old and tired from you pulling it all the time," he said. Though the truth was that when he was alone he liked to lie on his bed or sit at his window and suck on it. It was not a new habit; he'd had it since he was a little boy. It gave him comfort, or something close to it, and for a few minutes it lent his foggy mind a rare clarity: it took him back to the days of his childhood, to memories of his dead wife, Sarojini, and lately, to an understanding of something less pleasant, less wistful, but more necessary: it reminded him that he was at the end, that the places his sixth finger took him were the farthest places—and the only places—he had left to go.

Another thing he had trouble remembering was what exactly he used to do: it was a cruel irony that Alok Debnath had mapped half the subcontinent in his long career as principal cartographer for the Indian Geographical Society but that oftentimes could not name his own street. All Alok Debnath could really recall was the feel of Rekha's body against his own. The chocolaty edges of her round buttocks pressing into his crotch, her skin sometimes smooth, sometimes rough from goose bumps he had caused, the cold had caused, or—as she was quick to point out—because she was thinking about her pimp, the only man she truly loved. "Your pimp," Alok Debnath asked her, "how could you love *him*?" She'd scoff, and say, "Who would you rather I loved? A limp drooling old fart like you?" It's all right, it's all right, he thought, gently stroking her hair. Her words didn't matter so long as her body lay next to his. But then she'd sit up and say, "Your time's up."

"But I paid for the entire day."

"No you didn't, you paid for two hours." Was she lying? She could easily do so and he would never be the wiser. "But," he'd begin . . . it was then that it all came back to him. In a way. His mind with its dark and empty recesses, the lost hours, the lost days, the confusion of starting for someplace and ending up in another, the horrible, horrible decay of age, entire years lost like a broken shoelace, and worst of all was when he looked in the mirror and the face looking back at him was unrecognizable, misshapen, and as battered as a bridge on the verge of collapse.

He was in Calcutta. It was a warm spring afternoon in 1920. Alok Debnath had been married for two months. His new bride, Sarojini, was a girl from a middle-class family in Jamshedpur, sweet and loving and awkward (since they had only met on the day of their wedding), with delicate dark gray eyes and lips as moist and plump as a bumblebee. He couldn't stop kissing them, and when he was away from her, which was most of the day, he would trace their shape onto the maps strewn across his desk, trying to find the perfect constellation of cities that matched her lips. Sometimes, though he tried not to, he thought of those lips sucking on his sixth finger. It was nothing he'd ever ask her to do, it was his deepest secret, but it made him almost cry to think of the simplicity of the gesture, the great intimacy of such a small and awful thing.

At the time Sarojini worked as a typist in a municipal government office. They had decided she should work until he was promoted to senior cartographer, which he expected within a year or two. She was fine with the arrangement, though she was new to the city and so every day at 6:00 p.m. Alok left his office at 45 Ballygunge Circular Road, walked to her office near Lansdowne Market, and then they walked together to their flat by Elgin Park. It was, for both of them, their favorite part of the day. But on this warm spring afternoon Alok was held up in a meeting, and by the time he got to Lansdowne Market it was 7:30 p.m. and Sarojini was gone. He went back to their flat, assuming she had come straight home, but she wasn't there either. He waited a few minutes then set out again, imagining the worst, not knowing where to begin, but determined to find her. Under his breath he said, "I'm coming, Sarojini, I'm coming for you."

He wandered out of Taktakpur, walking aimlessly but drifting toward the ghats. He'd only been living with his daughter for six months, since his diagnosis, and had never been to the shores of the Ganga. But he knew there were slums along the ghats and that Rekha lived in one of them. That's all she ever talked about: living with her beloved pimp on the western edge of the Dharahara Mosque, near Pancha Ganga Ghat, but Alok Debnath didn't get much past the Arabic School before he felt hungry. He walked into a restaurant, the first he saw, and ordered vegetable biryani, chicken 65, and a mango lassi. He ate with great relish, the sour sweet creaminess of the lassi a frigate to the spicy sting of the chicken. When he had finished his meal and the waiter brought the bill, Alok Debnath checked his pockets. They were empty. He checked them again and when he found they were still empty, he sat, perplexed. "Somebody stole my wallet," he said.

The waiter laughed. "Is that right, old man," he said. "And I bet somebody stole your mama's chutia too." He stopped laughing. "Pay up."

Alok Debnath looked at him helplessly. Where could his wallet have gone? The waiter reached down and grabbed him by the lapel, shaking him. A diner at the next table intervened. "What's the problem?" he asked.

"These old people," the waiter said. "They think they can pull this little act and get out of paying."

The diner asked how much the bill was for and paid it along with his own. By now Alok Debnath was shaking. The wrinkles under his eyes were wet with tears. The diner helped him up and when they got outside he asked where he was going. Alok Debnath looked at his hands and honestly could not remember. He concentrated hard for a moment. "Ah," he said, "I'm going to look for my wife."

"Where is she?" the diner asked.

He looked again at his hands. He didn't recognize them; they were the hands of an old man. "She works near here, near Lansdowne Market," he said.

The diner looked at him strangely. "Come to my house," he said. "You can have a nice cup of chai and then we'll figure things out."

"No, no, no," Alok Debnath said. "I have to find her, there's no time to waste." He was nearly at the corner when the diner ran after him, put a rupee coin in his hand, and said, "Go with God." Alok Debnath looked at the coin and dropped it into his pocket. A few steps later, when a thin beggar girl approached him, her eyes as bright and beautiful as lamps, he dug in his pockets, pulled out the coin, and gave it to her.

* * *

Alok retraced his steps back to his office. His wife was nowhere along their usual route. He looked in every shop,
around every stall, ran up and down stairs; he even looked
under the road crossings. The perspiration gathered under his
arms, his heart raced. He told himself, Calm down, you
won't find her unless you calm down. Then he said to himself, She's been in Calcutta for two months, she certainly
knows the way home. With this thought he seated himself
beneath the Corinthian columns of his office building. The
russet-colored walls, under the twilit sky, shone like stripped
bark. He could imagine sap running down their lengths.
The palm trees swayed and bent with the wind. And even the
sky seemed strangely blushing or bruised, as though just
then, in that instant, it had learned what it was to have a face
only to have it promptly punched. He thought of Sarojini
with sudden despair. She was lost. He could feel it. He could
feel her wandering alone in this vast city as well as he could
feel his own breath. He leapt up. He raced to Maddox Square.
He didn't know what he expected to find but there was nothing, only an open field. There was a boy sitting next to a
monkey. A few men loitered on the edge of the field, smoking. He heard the cries of boys playing cricket in an adjoin-
ing field. He turned back to the boy and the monkey. The boy
was wearing a cotton shirt and a lungi, and there was a pan in
front of him and around this pan danced the monkey. She
(Alok presumed) was wearing a little frock, just the kind of
frock a little girl would wear. In fact, it probably *was* a child's
frock. It had been pink but was now dirty and stained and

a dull gray. The boy looked up at him, the monkey stopped dancing, and she too looked up at him. The monkey's eyes were curious but the boy's were blank. "Do you want to see a trick?" the boy asked.

"What can she do?"

"She can tell your future," he said.

Alok laughed. "My future then," he said.

"First the money," the boy said.

Alok dug into his pocket and all he had was an eight-anna coin, the rest were rupee notes. The coin clanged when he put it into the pan. The monkey, at the sound of the clang, sprang into action as if she were a windup toy. She danced a little jig, ran to and fro, then she took the coin Alok had placed in the pan and put it in her mouth. "She's swallowed it." He chuckled.

"No she hasn't," the boy said, "she's telling your future."

"Well, what is it?"

"You'll soon see death," the boy said.

Alok's heart buckled. Sarojini! "You lie," he screamed back as he ran. "You and that damned monkey." The boy looked away but the monkey stood still, watching him, and seemed to smile.

Benares was dark by the time Alok Debnath found himself in Nadesar Park. He continued wandering down Raja Bazar Road and then onto the grounds of the Sanskrit University. He sat on the edge of the fountain with the stone swans and began to cry. He felt as lost and as afraid as a child. He thought of his mother. When he was six years old she had taken him shopping with her one evening. She had bought vegetables for dinner, eggplant and potatoes and ginger, a few sprigs of cilantro, and when he had tugged at her sari and asked her to buy him a pomegranate, she'd said, "No, not today, I don't have time to take out all those seeds for you." They had squabbled for a moment and finally she had given in and said, "If I buy it for you you'll have to take them out yourself."

He'd stood defiant—all six years of him—and said, "I will."

"You will," she said.

"I will."

"Promise?"

"I promise," he said.

She had bought the pomegranate and as they walked home Alok had let go of her hand to watch a snake charmer on the side of the road, and as the snake had emerged from the basket a landaulet turned the corner and one of the horses reared in fright and the other horse swung to the side and caught his mother's rib, and by the time Alok understood enough to run to her she was dead. A crowd had gathered. Two British women who had gotten down from the landaulet were shielding their faces, sobbing, and repeating, Oh dear, oh dear, oh dear. All the other people around his mother were Indians, peasants, and they looked on silently. Alok turned from them to his mother and saw that the pomegranate had rolled and been crushed, and was lying at the tip of his mother's outstretched hand. It looked to him like she was taking out the seeds for him, after all. He walked to the middle of the circle of onlookers, bent down, picked up the pomegranate and began to eat it. A man standing beside him slapped him. "How dare you," he said. What could Alok say? Not even he understood. It took him many years, more than twenty, to finally figure out the reasons he had picked up the pomegranate and eaten it in the moment of his mother's death: he had wanted to make her proud, to show her that he could, that he knew, he *sensed*, even at the age of six, that he would never again be a child, and that nothing, not even her death, could keep him from continuing, from living— which is what she would have wanted—and that, most important of all, he, Alok Debnath, her son, would always, always keep his promises.

Alok Debnath looked up from his tears but the swans stared back without a sound. "What's wrong with you?" he shouted at them. And then he said to himself, Why couldn't I be made of stone. A gust of cold wind whipped past him and he tugged his coat closer. He turned around. Behind him was the main university building—red and Gothic and leaping into the dark night like a tongue of flame. Its portico was protected from the wind and he crawled into one of its far corners and drifted to sleep. He dreamed that somebody was tugging at his sixth finger and he mumbled, "Bunny, stop it."

He ran and ran and ran. All of Calcutta, all of India, every little boy and every little monkey, filled him with rage. They would not take another woman from him. He wouldn't let them; he forbade it. He returned to Lansdowne Road, looked wildly about him, and decided Sarojini had gone to the Victoria Memorial. They liked to go to the building site on Sundays to see what had been added. It was like watching the Taj Mahal being built. Then they'd sit on the banks of the Hooghly and eat roasted peanuts. All this whizzed through his mind—the peanuts, the river, the Taj Mahal—as he raced up Lansdowne, across Elgin Road, and then north on Chowringhee Road in a hired rickshaw.

It was dark by the time the rickshaw wallah pulled onto Queen's Way. The Victoria Memorial glowed like a white hot candle against the warm night sky. He raced to their usual spot: a sort of pier that was built along the reflecting pool. The wooden boards clattered and shook as he raced up and down the viewing area, but she wasn't there. She wasn't there. Alok crumpled onto the pier, the water in the reflecting pool lapping gently at his hunched body. He cried out, "Sarojini!" The few people taking their after-dinner walks looked at him, and then moved away. One or two children hid behind their father's legs. The memorial seemed to flare with laughter, with its white and awful and treacherous teeth, as if it had conspired to hide her. Alok closed his eyes. The only thing left to do was to go home. But he couldn't face the empty rooms, not yet. He glanced at the reflecting pool and saw in the dim light that there was something at the bottom of the pool. A dark form. It couldn't be! He jumped in, stretched out his arms and tugged at the water. When he reached it he plunged deeper into the pool and lifted it tenderly with both hands, but it was only seaweed. Floating without a care on an enclosed body of water that was not at all connected to the sea. So how did it get there? Alok dropped it back into the water with a splash and let out a cry. It was a question that he too asked himself. So how did I get here? The answer, if there was one, seeming dizzyingly simple or dizzyingly complex. He turned back toward the pier and under the thin light of the stars the white marble of the moon and the white marble of the Victoria Memorial were the same, as if one had been chiseled from the other, and they bathed his dripping body in a pearl-like luminescence.

"Hey, hey, get out of there." It was a chowkidar, standing on the edge of the pier.

Alok stopped.

"Hey, you, I'm talking to you. What are you? Deaf?"

He recognized him. He had a paunch, and a handlebar mustache. He patrolled on Sundays.

"I know you! Have you seen my wife?" Alok yelled back.

"Your what? I said get out of there."

"My wife." Alok took long strides toward the pier. When he reached it he stayed in the pool and looked up at the chowkidar. "My wife," he said. "We come here sometimes on Sundays."

"Get out of there, I say." He looked up. "Pagal! You'd think it was a full moon tonight."

They were silent.

"How did that seaweed get there?" Alok asked.

"Seaweed? What seaweed?"

Alok pointed to it. The chowkidar arched his neck to have a look. "That's seaweed?" he asked. "Looks like a crocodile."

"It's not. It's seaweed."

The chowkidar shrugged. "Who cares," he said. "Get out of there before I have to come in after you."

Alok Debnath left the grounds of the Sanskrit University. He guessed it was between 2:00 and 3:00 a.m. It was a moonless night. Most of the streetlights were burned out. Why are the streetlights burned out? he asked himself. What is the year, what is my name? "My name is Alok Debnath," he said into the dark. "I am eighty-four years old, the year is 1976, the year of Indira Gandhi's Emergency, and that's why the streetlights are burned out." This series of thoughts, instead of making him less anxious, made him more anxious: What am I doing out here in the middle of the night? He could practically taste the river now. Such a mighty river, the mightiest. He'd mapped it so many times—it and its tributaries—that he could lay down against its twists and turns as if it were the body of a woman. That's it, that's why I'm out here: I'm looking for Rekha! His sense of purpose was renewed and he increased his pace, roughly following St. Kabir Road. By the time he got to the Durga Mandir he was exhausted. He sat on the steps of the orange and ochre temple and wondered which direction Pancha Ganga Ghat was in. He couldn't possibly know. He decided instead to head straight for the river and to then look for the ghat.

As he neared the river the alleyways narrowed. They cut into one another, some ended abruptly; the smell of incense was thick in the passages, most no wider than he was. Holes were cut into several of the walls along the corridors, and when he ducked into one he saw that it was a temple, small and dank and flooded with red and golden light. A young Brahmin was in the interior, chanting prayers, petals drifting down the deity's jewels and silks and landing at the priest's feet. Alok Debnath folded his hands and said a prayer. "May I find her," he whispered, and edged out of the tiny opening. He stepped back into the passageway. He passed a niche cut into a stone wall with a seated Ganesh, his belly rubbed bright red with kumkum, and then another temple, with an old sadhu sleeping under its eaves, and then the horizon seemed to lighten but no, it was the river. Alok Debnath looked out at the Ganga. There were a few small white swells on its surface but mostly it was gray, with a sandbar peeping above the water in the distance. He heard the water lapping against the stone steps. People were huddled and sleeping, and not wanting to wake them, he stepped around them gingerly. He noticed with dismay that all the slums—where Rekha most likely had lived—had been razed. Gandhi had taken care of them as well as the streetlights, but it no longer mattered, he felt lucid. He felt more lucid than he had in years.

It was as he was standing on the Brahma Ghat that Alok Debnath was approached by a young man. He could tell he was young by his voice. He could also tell he was thin. It was still too dark to see him clearly, though when the man struck a match to light his beedi, Alok Debnath saw his betel nut-stained lips, the dark hollows of his eyes, and the flash of greed in them. Remember them, he told himself, remember his greedy eyes.

"Where are you off to, grandpa? A little early for bathing, isn't it?"

"I'm not bathing," Alok Debnath said.

"Oh?"

What was it he was supposed to remember? He scratched his head. "I'm looking for someone," he finally said.

The young man slapped his shoulder. He took a drag of his beedi. "I'm your man," he said. "I know everyone from here to Sarnath. Who is it?"

"Her name is Rekha."

"Rekha! I know hundreds of Rekhas. Give me a little more, grandpa."

The red glow from the man's beedi pulsed like a warning. Alok Debnath hesitated. He could describe her, sure, but it would be a description of her ass. The tiny dimples, the downy hairs, and oh, the exquisite roundness of it. "She's a young woman," he said.

The young man laughed. "Compared to you everyone is young."

"She said she lived in Pancha Ganga Ghat, on the western edge of the mosque."

"Servant?"

"No."

"Whore?"

The young man let out a puff of smoke. Even in the dark Alok Debnath could see his smirk. "Pancha Ganga, you say?"

"Near the mosque."

He thought for a moment. His voice lifted. "What is her pimp's name? Naagi?" He didn't wait for a response. "Follow me," he said. They plunged back into the labyrinth of alleyways. They walked away from the river. Deeper and deeper into the incense-choked passages. The alleys grew narrower, more breathless in the looming dark. Shouldn't it be morning by now? Alok Debnath struggled to keep up. His feet ached. His lungs burned. He wanted to tell this strange man to stop, to tell him he wanted to go home, to tell him he had never felt so lonely. "What's the matter, grandpa? Can't keep up?" The man laughed and pulled him along. A rat scurried past. Alok Debnath stopped. "No, no, no," he heard the young man saying. "You can't turn back now. We're almost there." The close alleyway was still dark, doors and windows were shuttered on either side, but when he looked up, Alok Debnath noticed that the sky had lightened. Just a little. Just enough. It's morning, he thought with relief, it's almost over.

Alok left the Victoria Memorial, dripping wet, and walked along Cathedral Road back down to Chowringhee. He stopped in Elgin Park. It was near their flat, and he was exhausted, and the night was cool. There were no benches in the park—just a strip of grass and some trees. He walked to its center and sat cross-legged on the grass. A goat walked toward him. There was a high iron fence around the park, and Alok wondered how the goat had gotten in. Through the gates, like anybody else, he guessed. Maybe it had jumped over the fence. It seemed miraculous to him: that a ridiculous-looking creature like a goat could sail gracefully over such a high fence. It ambled over to him and stared at him with a forlorn look in its eyes, as if Alok were sitting on the juiciest patch of grass in all of India. "Come now," Alok said to the goat, "you can't want *this* exact patch, can you?" The goat blinked and continued with its sad stare. "Fine," he said, giving in and getting up. He was dusting off his pants—their dampness had collected every dry blade of grass and dirt in the vicinity—when he felt a tap on his shoulder. It was Sarojini.

"My God," he cried, and took her in his arms and pressed her close to him. He had never done so in public, had never so much as touched her, but what did it matter? She was here, in his arms. He wanted to ask her a million questions, but the goat was still watching them. He took her hand and said, "Come, he'll start crying if we don't leave this patch of grass." She laughed, and it seemed to him that he'd never really heard her laugh before. They settled themselves under a neighboring chalta tree. "Look here," he began, "Where—"

"You're soaking wet," she said in alarm.

He thought he might explain to her one night about jumping into the reflecting pool and the seaweed and the boy and his monkey that told his future (wrongly, he thought gleefully) but not tonight. Tonight he held her under the chalta tree and watched the stars.

* * *

The young man turned into an alley that ended abruptly at a green wooden door. He knocked twice. Alok Debnath rested his hand against the wall and it came back wet. A stinking sewer sloshed past them. He looked up and saw the mosque. After a few moments they heard footsteps and the door opened. The person who had opened the door hid behind it, though by now Alok Debnath's vertigo had traveled up his body and reached his eyes. The close dark veranda they entered swam before him and he collapsed into a nearby chair. The young man spoke in whispers to a fat wheezing man who'd emerged from the inside of the house. He was smoking a cigarette. A rare American cigarette. Alok Debnath could tell from the smell. After the fat man went back inside the young man sauntered over to him and asked, "Tired?" His voice was more frightening than solicitous.

"No, I want to go home."

The man smiled. "What about Rekha?"

"Who's Rekha?"

The young man eyed him suspiciously. A voice called from an interior room, "Bring him in." Alok Debnath made no move to get up. The man grabbed him under the arm and pulled him up by force. They entered a small room lit by a kerosene lantern. It was cold. There was an overhead light, just a bulb swaying at the end of twisted wires, but it was unlit. The fat wheezing man was in the corner. Another man, younger and thinner, sat at the table that held the lantern. He was wearing a dirty undershirt, soiled yellow. His eyes too were yellow, as if he was jaundiced, but his face was perfectly calm. Even happy. He looked with what seemed like true delight at Alok Debnath and he motioned with his arm. "Come, come, sit here, old man, sit by me." His arm, as it motioned, bulged with muscle. His face twisted into a smile. Alok Debnath sat opposite him, and that is when the man's other arm emerged from under the table holding a knife. He laughed. "Oh this," he said. "Don't mind this, old man, just a bad habit of mine. I'm Naagi," he added jovially. "The little bird who brought you here says you're looking for someone."

"Yes," Alok Debnath said. "I'm looking for my wife."

There was silence. "Your wife? He didn't say anything about your wife." Alok Debnath turned to look but the young man he'd come with was gone. It was only he, the fat man, and the man with the knife left in the room. They seemed to be waiting, so Alok Debnath waited with them. The young man returned a few minutes later with a woman. The moment she saw Alok Debnath she squealed with surprise. "You," she said. "What are *you* doing here?"

"He says he's looking for his wife," the fat man said.

She walked past him and Alok Debnath, with a small inexplicable glimmer of joy, looked at her ass. She stood behind the man with the knife. "Don't mind him," she said. "He's a crazy old coot. His wife's been dead for twenty years." Alok Debnath nearly wept at these words. Where was Sarojini? Who were these people? Why did they say she was dead?

"But his daughter," the woman continued, "now *she* is loaded. Lives in the biggest house in Taktakpur."

"Taktakpur?"

The man laid down his knife. His eyes widened, he turned to the woman. "Is that right?" he said. He relished each word, as if they left the taste of money on his tongue. He studied Alok Debnath with a smile on his face. Then he turned back to the woman and yanked at her arm until their heads were together. He whispered into her ear. She nodded excitedly and said, "Yes, yes. Ji, yes. I'll go there first thing," she said.

They both looked at Alok Debnath. The woman smiled maliciously but the man looked at him with benevolence. "It's all up to your daughter now," he said. "Get comfortable, put your feet up. Rekha, bring the man some water!"

Rekha. The name was vaguely familiar. Maybe he was mistaken, maybe he knew these people from long ago. He gripped the table and tried hard to focus. A sliver of light seeped through a crack in the wall. It was the sun. "It's the eastern edge of the mosque," Alok Debnath said. "You told me it was the western."

"What?"

"When I asked where you lived. You said the western edge of the mosque. But look," he said, pointing to the shard of sunlight.

The woman named Rekha ignored him and turned to the man. "We should send something with the note. Something to prove we actually have him, and no one else."

The man nodded. He picked up his knife. "But what?" he said.

They all seemed to look at Alok Debnath's right hand at once. He whipped his hands off the table and jumped away so quickly that the lantern went out with a crash. He turned to flee, but the fat man was already at his side, clutching both his wrists. Then everything seemed to fall at once: Alok Debnath back into his chair, his right hand back onto the table, and his senses back into place. No, these were strangers, they were criminals, and they were cruel.

The woman switched the lightbulb on but it remained dark. She lit a candle, turned it over so that the hot wax dribbled onto the table, then anchored the candle on the soft wax. The light was flickering but it was enough. The fat man still held him by the wrist. Alok Debnath's sixth finger stuck out toward the man and his knife as if it didn't have a care in the world. As if it had already gone on and made a life for itself separate from his own. He thought then of how dark it was in Elgin Park. Had they fallen asleep? He didn't know but when he opened his eyes, his new bride had taken his sixth finger into her mouth. He barely breathed. It was the greatest pleasure he had ever known. And yet he was still aware of everything around him. The branches of the chalta tree rustling in the breeze, he sensing their soft swaying above him. And the stars, the stars glimmering like distant bonfires. Too distant to light our world. And so there was no need to close his eyes again; it was dark. He could hardly even see her. Only feel the heat and wet of her mouth, the strength of her tongue.

Oh, my love, he thought, let there never again be light.

THE ROAD TO MIRPUR KHAS

My wife comes into the room, shutting out the sun as she closes the door, and lays the wad of bills on the table in front of me. I can't look at her. I want to feel shame but I only feel a thin pleasure, like a fine layer of skin, puckered and white and soulless, floating on cooling milk. On another shore, perhaps, the desert has an ashen end; and forests are merely silent folded wings. On that shore poverty doesn't have an animal stink. And when we touch the face of another, we draw onto their skin a moonlit path, and not the metallic rust of our weakness and our fear.

But on *this* shore, on this morning, there is only money.

She walks to the other end of the hut and lies down on the reed pallet, turned to the wall and silent, not even bothering with the blanket, as if she means to die like a wild animal. But at the sight of her hips desire floods me—not love, not any longer; love is simply a feeling that we walk off and forget at the side of the road, remembering it only hours later, and wondering—because we cannot go back, because we have come too far—at the lightness of our load.

The first of our money was stolen just after we left Jaisalmer. We were barely two days out but I could already see the row after row of mango trees waiting for us in Mirpur Khas, heavy and sagging with fruit. "It's harvest time," Ram had said. "They'll need workers bad, no telling how much they'll pay per bushel." But even as he'd said it he'd looked sidelong at Arya, bent low over the cooking fire, and I knew he was no longer thinking of the kind of mangoes that grow on trees. Still he was considerate enough: he gave me a month's wages for the journey, along with the name of a friend of his who owned an orchard. I'd tucked the money into the rusted Bournvita tin that held our savings, twenty rupees in all, along with the name of the orchard owner, and then wrapped it tightly in Arya's red woolen shawl. The first night I slept with the bundle under my head; the jasmine-scented coconut oil Arya used in her hair was a lullaby and I dreamed the most beautiful dreams. In one I was standing under a waterfall, laughing, my eyes narrowed, trying to distinguish between the water and the tiny sparrows that fluttered everywhere. It was almost as if the water, as soon as it hit my body, was turning *into* birds, their wings warm and quivering and soundless.

Then I woke and the money was gone. We'd gotten off the main road at nightfall and had found a sheltered spot under a grove of sangri trees. I'd lain awake most of the night listening to the desert sounds—the slither of lizards and snakes and the scurry of a few roaming gazelles—but I must've fallen into a deep sleep in the early morning hours. When I woke at daybreak the entire bundle was gone along with the chappals I'd placed in the hollow of a nearby tree. We had nothing left except the few rupees I'd folded into the tail of my dhoti. And we had at least a two or three weeks' journey remaining to get to Mirpur Khas; now we'd have to do it barefoot.

She's stopped speaking to me. At times the silence is so deep that I can hear the howl of distant jackals, and I'm reminded of the mangoes hanging in faraway orchards, their tough unscarred skins so unlike—so unlike what?—I don't know, I suppose my own.

I'd searched for the bundle: I'd left Arya crying as I climbed and slipped across the endless sand dunes. I knew the twenty rupees would be gone, certainly, but maybe they'd thrown off the shawl or the chappals, cracked as they were, the soles full of holes. I walked for a mile or two in either direction, scanning the dunes. I even looked inside foxholes and in the branches of scrubs. Nothing.

It was when I returned later that morning that Arya had pointed at the ground. "Look," she'd said, indicating a scatter of footprints near the area where we'd slept. "We know they're not ours. *These* people had shoes."

I looked at her. It was the first time since we'd been married—barely six months ago—that she'd spoken to me with such distaste. We'd not once quarreled in all that time. Nor had she ever looked at me like she looked at me then: her eyes shadowed, disappointed, full of fire and sadness, and something I cannot describe, maybe the ache of being without shoes, in the desert, her husband poor and useless, drawn by the jasmine-scented dream she did not have.

She turned and walked away from me. Toward what, I wondered. Yet I didn't call out. The wind pushed the lilac fabric of her shalwar tight against her body. The round of her hips, the gentle curve of her back made me shudder. I watched as she scrambled up a particularly steep sand dune, her chunni fluttering behind her like a torn sail, her arms outstretched to keep balance. And it was these arms; I seemed to be seeing them for the first time. Thin, almost twigs, balancing so bravely against the force of wind and sand and steepness. Angling to right themselves, pushing forward. The sleeve of her shalwar reaching just past her elbows and the brown of her forearm emerging as smooth as a new branch. Flowers have sprouted from less.

But then she fell. Arms first. She rolled down a ways, stopped, gathered her chunni around her shoulders, pulled her knees to her chest in the trampled sand, and simply sat there. No expression on her face. I watched her for a moment but she didn't move, as if she was determined to be as indelible and as piercing as the line of ridge above her.

I thought then of our wedding night and how, when she'd entered the hut, she'd stood shyly in the shadows until I'd coaxed her into the candlelight. She hadn't looked up until I took her chin in my hand, and only then had she raised her eyes to me. She'd seemed a wisp of a girl, no more than a fledgling bird, and I'd been overcome with the thought that she was mine—this golden, candlelit face, these firm, ample breasts, and this dizzying fragility, so sweet and untouched.

She's lying on the reed pallet. The hut is dark though the sun must've crept higher, is no doubt slithering past the thatched roof. We'd found it abandoned a few days ago—one of so many huts abandoned during the riots, left for fear of being trapped inside, the smell of burning flesh always in the air, a reminder to keep moving—all the pots and pans and mats and even some clothes were left behind. But we have decided to stay. The location is ideal: the lorries stop just a few yards away. It is a way station for the drivers. They sleep in the cabs of their lorries and eat and wash at the collapsing shack nearby called Arun's Restaurant and Bar, a clearing of littered and drifting dirt with a few orange rattan tables scattered here and there. When we reached Arun's we could barely walk. We hadn't eaten for three days. Hadn't drunk a drop of water in two. I had none left for sweat, my feet dragged along the dirt. I begged the owner for some water, food. A morsel. Anything. He looked at Arya—his eyes indifferent, his teeth rotting and green near the gum line, the hairs on his ears thick as wiring—and said, "Anything?"

It was then that I heard it. A sound I will never forget: the quacking of ducks. We were in the desert—Arya beside me, the owner chewing on a gob of betel nut—and yet the sound was as clear as if I were standing on the edge of a lake. I'd heard of inland seas, and pools that spring silently in secret, forgotten ways. And even in my weakness I imagined standing on its shore. The ducks rising, the flap of their wings. I imagined them gliding along on the unruffled waters. And yet it was the sound—their quacking—that gave me hope. That stilled my sorrow. And I knew then that this suffering—this dumb and gleaming suffering—wouldn't be the only language with which we'd speak.

Arya moved quickly in front of me, her face defiant with hunger, and said, "Anything."

They disappeared behind the screen, to the back of the restaurant. It was strange, how intently I watched that screen. I don't know why; it was so ordinary. Just woven jute that was quite battered and faded from the sun. And yet it held my attention with such force that I nearly knelt in front of it with a keen and baffled reverence. A small hole, punched into the top right-hand corner and no larger than a mango, was particularly captivating. How did it get there? Maybe rats had chewed through it but how could they have climbed so high? And to what end? The streaks of light that passed through it: was it the sun or an interior lamp? And how focused, that light, almost as if it were trying to indicate some truth, some error. But then I blinked, or something essential calmly passed before me, and the effect was gone. I couldn't understand it. It was a plain old jute screen again, as it had always been, but I was so bereft I could've wept.

I stood there, unable to move, staring at that awful hole

in the jute screen—the light now sickly and quailed—when Arya returned. She held out four roti and some day-old cactus curry to me. Her hands were steady but mine, when I reached for the food, were trembling.

We lost the rest of the money soon after the bundle. We'd kept moving. We heard from others on the road to Mirpur Khas that riots had destroyed most of Jaisalmer, and very likely our hut on the outskirts of town had been burned to the ground. I cried when I heard this; Arya didn't even wince. At a crossing I suggested buying chappals but she said no. "What will we eat if we waste money on chappals?" she'd asked, picking out the tiny grains of sand and pebbles lodged in the cracks of her heels. So we kept walking.

On the morning of the third day a lorry pulled over on the side of the road in front of us. The driver, thin, wiry, eyes bloodshot from driving through the night, face and hair gritty and browned by the sun, slid his eyes over Arya and offered us a ride to the border, still a week's walk away. His name was Mohammed. "No, no, no," he protested when we declined, his mouth red and seeping with betel nut. "How can I allow my sister to walk all that way. She is too delicate, nah?" He nudged me, smiling, and I smiled back though I knew he was mocking me. Arya glanced at me nervously. When we had a moment alone she whispered, "But we don't even know him. What if he leaves us at the side of the road?"

"We won't be any worse off than we are now. Besides," I said, "I'll protect you." She bent her head and I knew she was thinking of the twenty rupees. We could've taken a bus with that money—neither one of us had ever been on one—or maybe even a train. I squeezed her hand as Mohammed urged us onto the seat beside him, smacking my shoulder jovially and chattering about the hordes of other refugees he'd seen crossing into Pakistan. "But none as unblemished as your fruit," he said, winking.

I helped Arya into the cab of the lorry even as my stomach tightened with a strange and gnawing hunger. I ignored it and for the first few hours we bumped along, the desert scrubs and sangri trees whizzing by. I'd never seen the desert in this way—seated high up in a lorry, the glass windshield between us. How different it looked. When we walked the desert seemed to unfold endlessly, and devouringly, like a bolt of cloth unfurling in all directions, which the slightest wind raised and flapped like the sides of a tent. And though it was overwhelming it was also oddly intimate. As if—even as we walked—we were a set of pins holding down the sides of this tent. But in the lorry it was merely a painting. It passed before us, and along us, and though the speed was exhilarating, I hardly recognized it. I tried to focus on something specific—a jojoba or khejri tree, a distant camel—but we were going so fast that it was instantly lost.

Once, when we slowed, I saw a red fox with a hare hanging limp in its mouth, drops of blood like a necklace on the sand. I pointed to it but Arya's eyes were closed. Occasionally we passed clumps of people on the road, bundles and small children balanced atop their heads or tucked under

their arms. I was watching a crowd of a dozen or so villagers, heading deeper into the Indian side, when Mohammed
pulled over. It was nearing twilight. A blue and steady darkness crept behind us, blanketing the dunes and the sprinkle
of shrubs and a distant clump of trees in shadow. I felt envy
for that shadowed stillness, rooted as it was, and always
would be, unaware of our passing.

The lorry came to a complete stop. Arya blinked her eyes
open. We got out to stretch our legs. Mohammed took me
aside. "Listen, bhai," he said, looking over his shoulder at
Arya, "we're running low on petrol. Maybe you could help
out, seeing as I'm driving you all that way for free." He
seemed to be studying the horizon as he spoke, as if he were
reading something that was written there. I watched him,
felt the handful of rupees hidden in my dhoti; the gnawing
in my stomach returned. Arya had gone off into the bushes,
the top of her head darker than the darkening shrub. The
desert stretched in every direction, shivering and forlorn
under the deepening sky.

We both looked down the length of road, barely visible
now except a thin white mist that crept silently along its
edges. He shuffled his feet. "Five will do," he said finally.

"Where will we get petrol this time of night?"

"There's a station not far from here." He climbed into the
lorry and pulled out a bag of stunted potatoes pocked and
nibbled through by rats. "Here," he said, holding them out
to me, "have her make these. I'll be back with roti."

I handed him the five rupees, thinking if we could just

get to the border I'd be certain to find work; we were Muslim, and we'd be in Pakistan, after all. He stuffed the notes into his shirt pocket, started up the lorry, and kicked up a cloud of dust in his wake. As soon as Mohammed started the engine Arya ran over to me from where she'd been waiting, in the dark beyond the headlights, too far for her to hear. "Where's he going?" she cried.

"To get petrol. Look what he gave us," I said, holding out the bag of rotting potatoes.

Her mouth twisted then in an ugly way. "You fool," she said coldly, turning away from me, "he's never coming back."

She didn't talk to me for the rest of the night. And though I laughed at her poutiness, in the end she was right: he never did.

We've been in the hut by Arun's Restaurant and Bar for five weeks now. I've grown almost fond of the low shack, hung with faded film posters and braided ropes of drying chilies. Sometimes I sit outside and order chai. I drink it slowly, under a khejri tree barely taller than me, watching the lorries come and go on the highway. The spattering of orange rattan chairs and tables in the courtyard—dusty and yellowed with sand—along with the withered grasses lining the road, are somehow comforting. They are familiar to me in a way that nothing else is; even the desert, though I've spent my whole life in its midst, has become a strange place. Its immensity aggravates everything, even the milk in my tea, and the khejri tree. The thin distant line of the horizon convulses with each passing lorry.

Still I wait, the afternoons drifting through my fingers like sand.

"Let's stay here," Arya said when we first arrived. "Just until we have enough money to hire a bullock cart." We've had enough money to do that for some time now. Then we decided to stay just long enough to have money to take the bus. Safer and quicker than the bullock cart, Arya reasoned. They wouldn't torch a bus full of people, she said. But now we've decided to stay until we have just enough money for a few nights lodging in Mirpur Khas. Just enough money, she keeps saying, just enough. I sometimes wonder—during the long hours alone in this hut or in the courtyard of Arun's—how much, exactly, that is. And how much it's already been.

She has a routine. She'll go out toward twilight, when the lorry drivers begin to pull into Arun's for the night. From the hut I can hear the rumble of their engines, the squeal of their brakes. I hear the slam of their carriage doors and I get that same gnawing in my stomach. It is a tightening so severe that my eyes water. I vomit bile. On some nights the pain is so awful that I sit near the latrines, out behind Arun's—the stench of urine combats the pain—and listen for the quacking of the ducks. That's the direction the sound had come from that first night. I've never heard it again but I've grown used to the scent of urine, so thick I can practically chew it like cud.

She comes back at daybreak and sleeps. She sleeps so long sometimes I think she'll never wake up.

That's when I watch her. Her breath steams the air between us. And her hips rise and fall, rise and fall. This morning I leave the wad of bills on the table and go toward her. But before I even reach her I smell the stink of other men. It's in her hair, under her fingernails. It is a wall, an ocean; it is a country I cannot cross. I want her more in that moment than I ever have before.

A week or so ago a car came along with two women and a driver. It was late in the evening. The desert around us lost in darkness. I was in the latrine behind Arun's. They stopped for tea and one of the women—short, with a slight limp, I could only see her silhouette in the dim starlight—began talking to someone wedged deeper in the darkness. It was Arya.

They talked in muffled tones for a few minutes until the limping woman coaxed Arya toward their table. "How long?" she asked.

"A few weeks."

The two women looked at each other. "You know he's not coming back."

Arya shrugged.

"We have a camp," the other woman said slowly, taller, her voice more tender. "It's for women like you, refugees, whose husbands have left them. They'll help you find your people."

"Besides, how long can you do *this*," the stout woman said, waving her hands vaguely toward the desert.

Arya turned her face. I saw it then in the half-light, angled toward a lorry that was pulling in. She looked at that lorry with such longing that even I thought she might be waiting for her husband to step down from it—hers, the one who'd once been brave, who'd once have stormed out from behind the latrines and called those women and their camp nakaams.

There was a long silence. The khejri tree under which they sat swayed as if to speak.

"No, I'm staying here," she finally said.

"But, beti," the taller one began, "what's left for you here? How long will you wait?"

Arya shrugged again. "As long as it takes," she said. Then she rose and trailed off after the lorry that had just pulled in. The women watched her go, clucking their disapproval. The tall one said, with a sigh, "These girls. They think their men will save them."

The short one laughed and the laugh rang through the desert quiet. "Pagals. They won't even come back for them."

"Why didn't you go to the camp?" I asked her the next morning.

I'd woken her up. I'd slammed pots and pans on the table. Pushed open the door of the hut. Sunlight streamed in and she blinked her eyes open, the irritation rising to her face after a moment of confusion.

"Close the door."

"Why didn't you go?"

"The door, you animal." She threw her pillow toward it, trying to catch its side and swing it shut. She missed.

"Why didn't you?"

"*What?*"

"Go. With those women."

She tossed away the blanket and gathered her hair in her hands. Then she pulled it into a knot at the top of her head. She stood up, shook out her clothes. I could see the rain of sand in the sunlight. She looked at the empty pots. "Didn't you make tea?"

"You could've gotten away."

She scoffed. She lifted a cup of water out of the vessel and drank it. "The least you could do is make tea," she said.

"Maybe even make a new life for yourself."

She threw the cup across the room. It struck the mud wall with a dull thud. Water streaked across the dirt floor; the steel cup gouged the opposite wall before clanging to the ground. Then it rolled toward me. I moved to pick it up. Arya turned and slumped into a chair. She bent her head and I thought maybe she'd fallen asleep again but after a long while she said, "Why bother? This one's lonely enough."

She'd cooked the rotting bag of potatoes and we'd eaten them. Then we'd slept together, huddled against the cold night air. When we woke, all those weeks ago, she'd looked at me sorrowfully and said, "Let's go back home."

"We can't."

"But *why?*" she'd asked, as if the answer would change.

I'd reached over and tucked a strand of hair behind her ear. I smiled; at least she was talking to me. "How much do we have left?"

I untied the end of my dhoti. I held the coins out to show her. "Eight annas."

"Let me have them."

"Why?" I said, looking at the empty dunes around us. "There's nothing to buy."

"You'll see," she said, and walked off in the direction we'd come.

I waited for a few minutes. When she emerged again on the crest of a near sand dune she had a milkweed flower in her braid. "Where's the money?" I asked.

"I buried it." She laughed. "We'll dig it up on our way back."

Our way back: how beautiful, that simple string of words. I looked past her; the honeyed scent of the milk-weed drifting between us. I thought then that perhaps life would never again be as exquisite as it was in that moment. With that cool early morning breeze. Sunlight, shy and tremulous, reaching for the curved body before it. And my Arya, my nymph, her eyes so hopeful and alive, raised to my own. And not an anna between us. As if—in the burying—she'd said, What need do we have for it? As if—in the burying—she'd said, When we have each other?

* * *

I make rice and dal. I set out a plate. I am quiet so as not to wake her. These days I have trouble sleeping, even during the hottest part of the afternoon. My thoughts wander through mango orchards, under the shade of their wide leathery leaves, and I think of the red woolen shawl. I think of how when I find it I will spread it under them. And how I will lie down in its jasmine-scented softness and close my eyes and fall into a deep and restful sleep. The deepest and most restful I have ever known. How I will dream again of waterfalls. And how I will wake, and Arya will smile. And no mango—in all of that orchard or in all the orchards of the world—will rival the sweetness of that smile.

For now I wander out toward Arun's. It's midday. The previous night's lorries have gone. New ones will stop here tonight. Everyone is asleep. There's no wind. I can almost hear the desert breathe. The rise and fall of its bosom. I can only walk in the shade and even then—even with the new chappals Arya bought for me—my feet burn from the heat of the sand. I settle against the side of the latrines, in an alcove protected from the sun.

I haven't eaten in two days. I haven't had a drop of water in over one. The sky above me twirls and spins. It is red and green and lilac and splinters like sparrows. I shut my eyes against its beauty.

I know the road to Mirpur Khas goes on for another hundred miles, and beyond that is Karachi, and beyond even that is the Arabian Sea. In Jaisalmer, they'd said, Go, they've made a new country for you. But all I can see is sand. And the only borders I know are the ones between our hearts.

I want to be hungry again. I want to arrive again at Arun's, like we did all those weeks ago. I want to be just as hungry, just as thirsty. I want to look into his indifferent face and I want him to ask again, "Anything?"

And this time I will step forward. Me. Not Arya. And this time, I will say, "Anything, except her."

The alcove too is now filled with light. My eyes blur with heat and tears. I see Arya, though how could it be? She's asleep. And yet she's bending over me and asking, over and over again, "Why? Why are you sitting here?" And then she draws her hand toward me and cries, "You're burning up, you fool. You're raging with fever. Come inside."

But I catch her arm. It's smooth and cool like alabaster. I want to cry into it, I want it to carry me, but instead I say, "Don't you hear them?"

She tugs. "Come inside."

"Don't you?"

"Hear what?"

I tilt my head toward the sky. "The ducks, of course."

She listens for a moment. Her eyes brim with tears, or maybe mine do. She lifts my chin as I'd once lifted hers. "Yes," she says finally, almost in a whisper. "Yes. I hear them."

The Memsahib

Before Arun opened his restaurant on Gadra Road—
the road that led to Mirpur Khas—he was a sweeper
and general coolie at the Palace Hotel in Jaipur. And before
that—from the ages of nineteen to twenty-one—he was a
servant at the home of British Army colonel Francis Chilcott on the colonel's estate outside of Lucknow. And about
the time before that, that distant childhood of his, Arun remembered nothing. The colonel had a fussy wife, Arun
thought, though he rarely saw her. Most days she stayed
firmly secluded in the shadowy parts of the house, ringing
the servants only when she wanted her jug of Pimm's refreshed in the summer, or more woolen blankets in the winter. She was gone for months at a time, jumping right quick
at any opportunity to board a ship for England. The colonel
had a grown son, Dicky, who'd joined the Indian Civil Service, and was home only on leave. He was jovial, arrogant,
rarely acknowledged the servants with more than a wave of
his hand, and the last time he'd been home he'd tripped over

Arun as he'd been cleaning the floor with a wet rag; Dicky had looked down at the kneeling Arun, both of them twenty years old, and had said, with a great and buoyant voice, "What a marvelous posture for you people. Really, you were quite made for it." The colonel had a daughter too, whose name was Lavinia, and it was Lavinia—beautiful, maddening Lavinia—who snuck nightly, still, into Arun's dreams, and hovered like death around his days.

He didn't see her for the first few months that he worked at the Chilcott home. She was at boarding school in Dharamsala, a place that the elite of the British Raj sent their daughters and that, as Colonel Chilcott complained to Mrs. Chilcott, "spoiled them worse than we do." The first time Arun saw her, she arrived for her winter holidays in a flurry of rickshaws and trunks and hatboxes and foreign-looking packages, finally emerging from the Durant her father had sent to the train station, clad in a yellow linen dress that seemed to Arun as thin and pearlescent as onion peel. She hurried past him, so close that Arun noticed a fine layer of perspiration on the ridge of her collarbone, and dainty pink spots on her throat that had brightened like petals in the winter sun. She trailed behind her a dusky scent—equal parts musk and frangipani and the just-departed monsoon. In fact, he thought afterward, she was much like the monsoon: billowing, vast, and the greatest relief for a parched and anguished earth. He could've stayed enveloped in her scent for the rest of his life but he was immediately dispatched to draw Miss Chilcott's bath. "Daddy," she was saying as he left the room, "why couldn't you send the car? That train was absolutely dreadful. The conductor was insolent *and* I saw an Indian sitting in first class. Just sitting there, Daddy."

That night Arun pulled the overhead punkah—not so much for the breeze as to keep away the mosquitoes—while the family gathered in the sitting room. Dicky was there, as well as Mrs. Chilcott. The dark teak of the floor gleamed in the lantern light, the crickets sang with full-throated delight.

"Shall we have Mr. Reed over, dear? Tomorrow, for tea?" Mrs. Chilcott said.

Lavinia yawned.

Arun's mother—who was the Chilcott's longtime cook and housemaid—came in carrying a tray with a bottle of port and four glasses. She set it down soundlessly on the center table. Then she glanced at Arun. He was watching Lavinia, the way her fingers wrapped delicately around the glass, the white of her skin like polished marble against the bloodred port. Earlier, in a moment of terrifying breathlessness, he'd caught a glimpse of a sliver of her bony knee as she'd folded her legs under her dressing gown.

"It's settled then," Mrs. Chilcott said. "I'll have Arun take a message over in the morning."

Lavinia sighed. "I wish my green silk were ready."

"The dressmaker said not for another week."

"The dressmaker," Dicky roared. "Why, you already have enough to fill Westminster Abbey. Besides, old Quince would propose to you if you had on a burlap sack."

Lavinia smiled, took a sip of her port, and looked at Arun. It was the first time she'd looked at him. Her eyes, in the lamp-light, were the green-gray of the Gomti on a clear day. Her face was the shape and color of a peeled almond. "Fetch me a sandwich, won't you? Something light. Cucumber, I think."

"Why, Lavinia," Mrs. Chilcott broke in, "you've just had your dinner."

"Leave her be, Georgette," Colonel Chilcott said. "The poor girl's traveled halfway across this country."

Lavinia sank back into the cushions of her chair and said, "Traveling does make one . . ." She trailed off when she noticed Arun watching her; she smiled at him, teasingly, as if she already knew he was in love with her, and she said, "Hungry." Then she raised a pretty eyebrow and said, "Don't you think?"

When Arun got to the kitchen his mother was putting away the dishes from dinner. He spoke in Hindi, trembling. "Chota memsahib wants a sandwich, ma."

His mother—old now, left by her husband when her children were still young, with two daughters she'd not seen since she got them married years ago, one in Kanpur and the other in Meerut, and having worked every day without fail for the past eighteen years—breathed deeply. She shook her head. "That girl," she said.

Arun grew angry. "Stop complaining," he said. "She's traveled half the country. It'll take two minutes."

His mother put down the knife she'd taken out to slice the cucumber. She was a head shorter than Arun and bent, her hair had gone completely gray, but for one instant—just that one last instant—she stood tall. "No, my son," she said. "She'll take more than that."

Arun delivered the message to Mr. Reed's butler the next morning. He considered crumpling it up and throwing it into the gutter but that was foolish; they'd realize immediately that he was at fault. Instead he settled for slipping the note into his kurta bottom and rubbing it against his genitals. By the time he returned, preparations for the tea were well under way. His mother was busy in the kitchen. The other servants were cleaning and sweeping and polishing every surface in the house, even the upstairs, where Mr. Reed was unlikely to go. Mrs. Chilcott was buried deep in her curtained room, hoping for an afternoon nap. Dicky and the colonel had gone to the club after lunch, promising Mrs. Chilcott again and again that they wouldn't be late for tea. And Lavinia was in her room. What was she doing? Arun wondered. He walked slowly by her door every few minutes, hoping to catch some sound or maybe even a glimpse. He was sure to take with him a candlestick or a dust cloth or a broom, in case he was caught out. He needn't have worried: the upstairs was eerily quiet. Mrs. Chilcott must have fallen asleep, and as for Lavinia, he was rewarded only once when, as he passed by her door, the linen yellow dress lay in a heap outside of it, presumably for the laundress. Arun looked up and down the hushed hallway, picked up the dress, and sniffed it. And there! There was that lingering smell of dusk, and railway dust, and coal, the soaring Himalayas, and just there, along the underarms, her true scent: pungent, animal, and so fugitive that he raised it to his mouth and sucked on it.

Mr. Reed arrived promptly at four, squawking his car horn. The servants were at attention. The sandwiches, cakes, and tea things were set out in the main hall, and Colonel Chilcott and Dicky were in the drawing room, reading *The Times of India*. By the time Mrs. Chilcott entered the drawing room, the three men were talking and joking about the Salt March. "Next thing you know they'll be walking all the way to London," Dicky said, laughing. Mrs. Chilcott settled into a wicker chair and told one of the servant girls to go and see if Miss Chilcott needed assistance. "The poor darling is so rightly famished, Mr. Reed," she said. "Train journeys in this country are abominable compared to English trains, don't you think?" They all nodded in agreement.

The harshness of the afternoon light dimmed, the tea was brought out, and Lavinia entered.

The men rose and each of them, including Arun, took a short intake of breath. She was ravishing: her chestnut hair was curled in a fashionable bob, she wore a simple yet elegant dress of silvery lilac, and her face—those Gomti eyes and moistened lips—shimmered in the last of the winter's light. Her arms were bare, soft and beautiful, and the slight translucent sleeves of her dress, resting like butterfly's wings against her shoulders, just hid them as they curved upward into her throat. And it was they—her shoulders—that Arun couldn't take his eyes from.

Mr. Reed approached her, kissed her hand. Arun bristled. Tea was poured and after some pleasantries, Mr. Reed invited Dicky and Lavinia to a garden party at the club the following week. "That sounds lovely"—Lavinia breathed—"*and* my green dress will be ready."

Colonel Chilcott had heard talk about a cricket match being organized, Dicky and Mr. Reed gave each other a look and said they didn't know of it. A cool breeze flowed through the windows and Lavinia pouted and said, "Why aren't we sitting on the veranda? It's too stuffy in here." Everyone was again in agreement and Arun was sent out to organize the tables and chairs. They shifted to the veranda, with the servants bringing the tea things and the colonel's pipe and cigarettes for Mr. Reed and Dicky. Once they had settled, talk resumed about the changes at the country club, and changes in the weather, and the changes needed in India's governance. But Arun heard none of it. He was concentrating with all his might on Lavinia's shoulders. Their lithe and hidden curves. Waiting, waiting, for the wind to conspire and raise her sleeve, just enough so that only he would see, only he would grow hard, and she would reveal herself, shyly, only to him.

The winter's deepening brought more garden parties for Mr. Reed and Dicky and Lavinia. All-day polo matches were organized at the country club, as well as a trip to a rest house on the outskirts of Mathura, and even an elephant race that held all the pomp and fanfare of the Royal Ascot. Mr. Reed, or Quincy, as the family began to call him, came and went almost daily. He and Dicky and Lavinia would stumble into

the house arm in arm in arm, laughing and singing and bois-
terous, full of youth and all its merriments. Most often,
unless he was addressed directly, Arun would leave the room
as quickly as possible and race back to the servants' quarters—
where he and his mother shared a room—and sulk. A few
times he cried. Once he broke a bell jar lantern in the main
hall and blamed it on a stray bird.

At the end of January, Mr. Reed and Lavinia announced
their engagement. It was a bright, clear day. It was warm
enough that Dicky told Arun to bring them nimbu pani.
They were gathered in the sitting room, and when Mr. Reed
told them Lavinia had honored him by saying yes, the family
broke into a loud cheer. "My dears," Mrs. Chilcott said,
"there's so much to do. When will you marry? Summer is
far too hot in this horrid place, perhaps the autumn?"

Mr. Reed glanced quickly at Dicky and then looked
down. "We, Lavinia and I, we were thinking of March."

"March?" Mrs. Chilcott said. "Did you hear that, Francis? There's so much to *buy*. How will I ever get to England
and back by March?"

The conversation went on and on in this way. It wasn't
until minutes later that Dicky noticed Arun standing very
still. "Didn't I tell you to bring us nimbu pani? What are you
doing, standing there? Hard of hearing?"

The sound of Dicky's voice was as if someone had knocked
him against the wall. Arun shook his head awkwardly, shuffled into the kitchen, and collapsed in a corner, weeping.
His mother ran to him. "What is it? What's wrong?"

Already his face was covered in tears. It was as though something had broken in him, as though something tucked behind the breastbone had shattered; something he had never even quite come to know, and had certainly never protected. His mother rushed to console him, not knowing what was wrong, and he managed to utter the words *nimbu pani*, and she understood only that much and left him, reluctantly, to prepare it.

That night he stumbled in the dark, unable to sleep. He walked around to the back of the house and looked out over the moonlit gardens. The damp shadows and pockets of blackness fit his mood. He drew blood when he pounded his fist against a stone bench. And the moon, what a traitorous moon: it was exactly the silver lilac of Lavinia's dress. He was walking along the garden wall at the side of the house when he noticed a small light, probably only a single candle, coming from Dicky's room. He was reading, Arun guessed, but then he heard voices. He crept along the wall and raised himself onto a ledge to see through the window. It was Mr. Reed and Dicky. They each had a drink in their hands, a whiskey maybe, and Dicky was walking around the room and Mr. Reed was sitting on the divan. Dicky was saying, "At the end of summer, I should say."

"That far away?"

Dicky looked at Mr. Reed and then he crossed the room and sat down next to him. He rubbed Mr. Reed's thigh and placed his drink on the floor, next to the divan. Arun stumbled backward. He stood still and out of the window came a small moan, and then another. Arun ran to his quarters. His mother was asleep. He looked at her: tiny, helpless, marked by the meanness of life. A life spent serving people who were no better than dogs, a life of being ordered around by them, cleaning up after them, being told to bring them fucking nimbu pani. And his poor sweet Lavinia, adrift in this sewage. She didn't even know! And so it was that his mother's sleeping, servile face gave him courage: he would get Lavinia alone, that's what he would do.

He waited a week for the right opportunity. She had just returned from the club. Dicky and Mr. Reed were still there, and would be arriving shortly. The colonel and Mrs. Chilcott were in Delhi attending a dinner at the Viceroy's House. She was in the drawing room. Arun entered it with sure strides, carrying a pot of tea and biscuits. He set it down in front of her. She was wearing a white blouse and a dark brown skirt. Her hair was done up with a satin bow. Though the sleeves of her blouse were long, Arun was able to make out the peak of her shoulder blade through the fabric. It was scintillating, the height of some great mountain pass.

"What is it? What are you looking at?"

She broke his reverie. Arun looked away but he realized he had to say it, how could he go on living without doing so? "I am—" he began, and then he fell silent.

She stared at him above her teacup. "Well, what is it?"

Arun heaved up his chest and concentrated on her shoulder. "I am . . . I am loving you, memsahib."

He dared not look at her but he felt a silence, unbearable in its weight, fall over the room. And then she broke it; she laughed. Not for very long, and not even very heartily. "How quaint," she said after a moment. "Now run along. Quincy and Dicky will be here soon and they'll be famished. Tell your mother to set an extra plate."

He turned to go but then he stopped. His eyes flashed. His body filled with something acrid. Searing. It was not that she'd been dismissive, it was not that she'd ordered him away, it was her laugh. So false, so unconvincing, so shabby; as if he were merely a child who'd done a little trick, and she only had to look up and feign amusement—and even then, not for very long—in order to satisfy him. He turned again and by now the rage was liquid, thicker than air. "Your Mr. Reed, memsahib, I must be telling you. He and Sahib Dicky—"

Her head shot up. "Don't you think I know that, you fool?" she seethed. Her face flushed redder than he'd known possible.

"But your marriage?" he stammered.

At this she was silent. The color drained from her face and there settled into her eyes a gray, stony light. "He's rich," she said. "He could buy you. He could buy a hundred of you."

"But, memsahib," and here he reached out to touch her shoulder, the very tip, not really knowing what he was doing, only wanting to reach her in some way, to convey a thing he could not speak. But before he reached it she swatted his hand away. "How dare you," she said. There seemed to be a slight struggle in her voice, the slightest hint of sorrow, but he knew it was for herself, not for him. "How dare you," she said again.

His humiliation was, of course, expected. But what he hadn't anticipated was his anger. He could hardly breathe. For his love to be called quaint, to be swatted away like a fly, to not even be *acknowledged*. It was too much. He walked through the rooms and did his chores with a deep and disturbing stoicism. He spit in her teacup, he came into her underclothes, he squeezed a drop of blood from his finger into her mulligatawny soup.

His mother noticed his distress but could do nothing. "Why don't you go visit your sisters," she suggested.

"Why?" he asked. "So I can see *their* servants' quarters?"

"It's our lot in life." His mother sighed.

"Shut your mouth. It's no lot of mine."

His mother was quiet for a moment and then she said, softly, "My son. Anger is a forest with no path."

He smiled. "She will know me."

"Who?" his mother asked. "Is this about chota memsahib?"

But he said nothing.

The true surprise came a week later when both Arun and his mother were dismissed. None of the Chilcott family was even home; they were told curtly by Mr. Chilcott's butler to leave the grounds of the estate by nightfall. "Hai Ram. What will we do?" Arun's mother wailed.

"Pack," he said.

"But why?" she cried. "You did something to her. Did you do something to her?"

He left their room without a word. He walked along the Gomti for hours. They had a few rupees saved; he could leave his mother with one of his sisters and then look for work. He would find a job in Lucknow, close to Lavinia. Maybe even in the country club, where he could see her daily. What was he watching her *for*, he wondered, but the thought left him as soon as it had come. What did it matter? These days Arun's thoughts, disturbing thoughts, thoughts that twisted into themselves and made no sense, he was able to shed as effortlessly as dead skin.

When he returned to their room, late in the evening, he was nearly joyous. His anger had found its source: his own weakness. The river had refreshed him, and Lavinia was his, his, his, and always would be. But when he opened the door to the room he found his mother lying on the ground. Their few clothes, some pots, and his bedding were spread around her. She was lying next to the hemp rope bed on which she slept. "Get up, Ma," he said, "I have a plan." She didn't move. He took two steps, to the middle of the room, and realized her body was strangely still. Arun let out a cry and plunged to her side, but she was already dead.

Arun sat alone in the dark. The butler had come by earlier to ask for the key but he'd taken one look at his mother's body on the floor and said, "You can stay till morning." Otherwise, no one came or went. He sat motionless; thoughts scampered through his mind like rats. Nothing settled, nothing stayed still. Not until deep into the night when he finally lit the oil lantern. He adjusted the wick and placed it on the ground next to him, between him and his mother. And that's when he saw it: that's when he saw the spider.

It—the spider—seemed to be staring at him. Well, it wasn't an *it*, he knew that much. It was a she. It was a female spider. And they stared at each other. It didn't take him long to realize what she had done; she had killed his mother. He could see the bite marks, the swollen upper arm. And he guessed at how it had happened: his mother had been pulling out a bundle from under the bed, a bundle they hadn't touched in months or years, and the spider had been dislodged by the disturbance and crawled onto her arm. It seemed to him—as they sat staring at each other—a perfectly reasonable thing to do. He might've done the same. In fact he felt a sudden kinship with the spider. He gazed at her with great regard, a kind of love, and he memorized the tiny details of her body—the thick yellow bands on her legs, the light underside of her belly, the stiff hairs covering her body—as if he were gazing into a lover's face.

When finally the spider began to crawl away, Arun watched it go and said, "Don't go too far." He waited till she'd reached her web, in a far corner under the bed, and then he too got up and left. By now it was morning, and flies had begun to gather around his mother's body.

* * *

He returned a fortnight later. He knew where the opening was in the wall that surrounded the estate, and he only had to push aside a few overgrown bushes to find it. He also knew that Lavinia would be alone; Mrs. Chilcott had already left for England, the colonel had stayed on in Delhi, and Dicky and Mr. Reed never returned from the club before eight o'clock. It was now a little after two and lunch would've already been served; the servants would have retired to their quarters for the afternoon.

He found her in the sitting room, reading. She must have gone riding, he guessed, because she was wearing jodhpurs and a long-sleeved cotton blouse. The punkah above her head moved listlessly in the slight breeze, the windows were thrown open. The afternoon light made the room seem to sway, as if it were a cabin on a tall ship. He entered it noiselessly, crouched and careful on the wood floor. He had with him a large quantity of rope, a rag, and a knife, and this last he pushed against her temple and said, "Nothing doing, memsahib." He then took the rag and stuffed it in her mouth and tied it behind her head. He told her to get up—the knife still grazing her skin—and pushed her out through the main hall and into the back garden, and then toward the servants' quarters, into the room he and his mother had shared.

The bed was pushed away from the wall and he shoved her onto it. He began tying each of her arms and feet to the bed. The first one—her right arm—was the hardest; she struggled, squirmed mightily, but he moved a knee onto her chest, and he pressed down harder until she looked like she might choke. By now he was besieged by her scent. They were so close his own pores seemed to emit it. Once he'd secured her to the bed he paused. He breathed deeply.

Then he knelt in the dark behind the bed and made sure she was still there. She was: her yellow-banded body was as exquisite as he remembered it. He looked into Lavinia's eyes, wide and fearful; he took his knife and sliced open her blouse at the shoulder. The fabric fell away and revealed to him that gentle curve, that lovely sea of cream on which he'd always sailed. He bent over it; his fingers hovered over its slight crest. He heard a groan and he rushed to console her. "Nahi. Nahi, memsahib. Not to worry," he said. "*That thing*, that thing I won't do."

He picked up the spider by the flat of his knife. He studied her. How beautiful, he thought, and then he thought, There is no end to the beauty and venom in women. Then he placed the spider on Lavinia's shoulder. The touch of the cold knife made her writhe but it was when she saw the spider that she leapt in terror, tugged against the ropes. Yelped with fear. But the spider held on, as he knew she would.

He went east. But first he locked the door of the room in which Lavinia lay. He walked along the Gomti. There was no one on the shore at this hour but he looked around, just once, before throwing in the key.

He arrived in Jaipur almost a month later. He'd walked most of the way. Sometimes there had been a bullock cart. A few miles of luxury on a freight train. But mostly he'd walked. He went to an ashram and bathed and ate a meal of dal and roti and potato curry. He heard from one of the other journeymen that the Palace Hotel was hiring, so he went the next morning to the hotel—a massive, glittering white building with blue shutters and bougainvillea—walked around to the back where the menial staff was congregated, and asked who he should see for a job. He was hired the following day as a cleaner, safaiwala, and all-around coolie.

It didn't take Arun long to note that most of the guests at the hotel were wealthy. He began, with this knowledge, working at his job quite earnestly and was soon promoted to the position of bellhop. After that it was only a matter of time—a week or so—before he opened an old British matron's luggage and found enough of what he was looking for.

He slipped the money into his bellhop's jacket, walked out of the main doors of the Palace Hotel, and headed east.

He paid cash for the Bikaner Rest House—a crumbling roadside stop that catered to lorry drivers—and renamed it Arun's Restaurant and Bar. He didn't care to change very much; he was happy with the low shack made of clay and jute, the walls hung with cinema posters. The only thing he added was a simple courtyard, facing the highway and cleared of scrub. He bought a few orange rattan tables and chairs, and planted a young khejri tree in the middle. He liked the way it looked: lonesome and emaciated, but alive.

* * *

The years passed. He remembered vaguely that he'd had a mother, perhaps some sisters. He remembered that he'd once worked in a large white building with blue shutters. He remembered a family of some sort, a dull, quiescent family whose recollection left him inexplicably agitated. He avoided memory. Instead he sat for hours on one or another of the orange rattan chairs, watching the highway, waving to lorry drivers, shielding his face from the sand and hot winds that rose and fell in the long afternoons. He thought this life suited him; that the emptiness of the desert was an emptiness he had always known. It was only rarely that he recognized anything more, that a layer or two would peel away. There was the time one of the lorry drivers asked if he served nimbu pani and for no reason he could understand, Arun felt a shiver run down his spine. And there was another time, just the other day, when he'd seen two people in the distance walking toward him. They were on the highway, in the heat of the afternoon, and they approached slowly. Maybe they were hungry. At one point one of them, maybe the woman, stumbled, and the man bent to help her up. She was on her hands and knees, and the man was bent at the waist, his arms reaching down to lift her. And in that moment, in that very instant, through the desert haze, there occurred to him the mirage of a creature with eight legs. A creature he had perhaps known long ago, one that was scented like dusk, and whose eyes had gleamed like the Gomti.

KAVITHA AND MUSTAFA

The train stopped abruptly, at 3:36 p.m., between stations, twenty miles from the Indian border, on the Pakistani side. Kavitha looked out of the window, in the heat of afternoon, and saw only scrubland, an endless yellow plain of dust and stunted trees, as far as the eye could see. She knew what this meant. One of the men in the berth, the tall one Kavitha had been eyeing, calmly told the women to take off all their jewels and valuables and put them in their shoes. "They'll search *everything*," he said with meaning, which made the young woman in the corner blush. Two or three of the women gasped. The old lady started crying. There were eleven people crowded into their berth, including Kavitha and her husband, Vinod. They were all from Islamabad, and had been squeezed onto the wooden benches of this train now for seven hours. There was an older couple that seemed to be traveling with their middle-aged son and his wife. The young woman in the corner was traveling with her mother and older brother. And the tall man was with his son, or so

Kavitha presumed, though they looked nothing alike. The boy was not more than eight or nine years old, but out of all of them, he seemed to remain the calmest, even more so than his father. He serenely took two thin pebbles, a curled length of twine, and a chit of paper, maybe a photograph, from his pockets and put them in his shoe.

They heard a clamor farther down the train, a few baleful screams then a series of thuds. Every door would be barred, they all knew, but when they were done looting the train, Kavitha hoped they would let it continue on as it was. She had heard stories, though: sometimes, they uncoupled the bogies and sent them in different directions. At other times, they forced the men to disembark and allowed the women and children to continue. More than once, she had heard, they boarded with kerosene. Kavitha reached out and took Vinod's hand. It was out of habit, she realized, but it was still a comfort. They had talked of this, now and then, in the course of their ten-year marriage: which one might die first. Kavitha had always insisted that she wanted to go first, that she could not possibly bear the pain of living without Vinod. But that was a lie. She knew very well she would manage just fine without him, maybe even better than she had. Their marriage, arranged by their families when she was sixteen and he twenty-two, and aside from one or two instances, had been mostly uneventful. Boring, really. He'd seemed handsome enough on the wedding dais, but when she took a long look at him, a week or so after the wedding, his forehead was squat, and his eyes were dull. As the months

went by, she noticed that the dullness persisted; they flick-
ered for a moment, maybe two, when he was on top of
her, but then they died out again. Dull eyes? her friends had
exclaimed. Just be happy he doesn't beat you. True, true,
Kavitha had agreed, but had secretly wondered if perhaps
that is what it would take to bring his gaze to life: violence.

There were four of them. The one who entered the berth first
had a distended ear, fanned out like a cabbage leaf, and was
clearly the leader. He stepped inside, holding a machete by
his side, by the handle, swinging it like a spray of flowers.
The others crowded behind him, holding sticks, and one a
metal rod. Now there were fifteen in the berth meant for six,
the heat growing even more unbearable, and the middle-aged
man, the one who was there with his wife and parents,
lunged, with a cry, at the metal bars of the train's windows,
trying to loosen them. It was pointless. They were welded in
place. His wife and mother tried to calm him but he was
weeping.
  "Look, how sweet," the leader said. "We have a baby in
the berth." The leader smiled serenely, looked at each of them
in turn, then put his hand on the shoulder of the man at the
barred window and said, "Here, let me help you." The man—
with a tremulous look, his face stained by tears, his hands
and shirtfront stained by the rust from the window—turned
and looked at him. "Come, come," the leader said, "let me
show you the way out." He pushed the others aside, and led
the man to the door. The man, still shaking, the surprise of

being led from the berth hardening into flight, took one quick look at his wife and parents and bolted out of the berth.

Cabbage Leaf smiled. "You see how easy that was," he said.

They stood in silence.

"Would any of *you* like to leave?" he asked. A fly buzzed. They waited motionless, as if they had all anticipated the sounds of the scuffle that reached them from the other end of the bogie, followed by a loud thump, a scream, and then a strange and preternatural quiet. The old lady—the mother of the man who'd left the berth—let out a long, piercing wail. "Now, now," the leader said, "there's no need for that." Then his voice dropped, it grew fangs. "Your jewels," he said.

It was a rainy afternoon. Kavitha was at home, preparing the evening meal of roti and dal with spinach and sweet buttermilk. Vinod was the tax collector for the district of Taxila, and was home no later than eight every night. She sweetened the buttermilk because Vinod preferred sweet buttermilk to salty, and she didn't have a preference. In fact, in the time since they had been married, it seemed to her that she'd lost most of her preferences. She had once liked taking evening walks, but he'd always said he was too tired. She had liked weaving jasmine into her hair, but the scent had made him nauseated. When she noticed fallen eyelashes on her cheeks, she'd put them on the back of her palm, close her eyes, and make a wish. Then she'd blow on them. If they flew away, she liked to think the wish would come true. If not, she'd wait patiently for another eyelash. She'd believed this since she was a child. He noticed her once, collecting the eyelash, blowing it away, and asked her what she was doing. He hardly ever asked her about herself, so Kavitha looked at him, astonished, then talked for ten minutes about the eyelashes, and the wishes, and the waits, sometimes lengthy, for the next one.

Vinod's eyes seemed to flicker—or so she thought—and then he frowned.

"What is it?" she asked.

"That's the most ridiculous thing I've ever heard," he said. "It's just plain silly."

"So what?" Kavitha said. "I'm not asking you to do it." It was the first time she had talked back to him, and she felt good for having done it.

That was when he slapped her. Not hard, but just enough so that she understood. Understood what, she wondered. She looked, in the instant after the slap, into his eyes. They were empty. Not a flicker. Not a sign of anger, or regret, or even satisfaction. She looked down. She too felt empty.

That was years ago.

On this night, after preparing the evening meal, Kavitha sat at the window of their flat. Vinod would be home in an hour. The window was big and looked out onto a row of facing flats, and most clearly into the flat directly opposite. A young couple lived in it, Kavitha had noticed, and she liked to watch them especially. This was about the time the young husband was due home, and Kavitha waited anxiously for his arrival. It was not that they were ever lewd or inappropriate, or even that they did anything interesting or unusual; it was just that there was such sweetness between them. She could tell just by their gestures, by how they moved, by how their bodies seemed to lighten the moment the other walked through the door. On previous afternoons, she'd noticed that the young wife wore a plain, cotton sari during the day, and just before her husband was to arrive, she would change into a more colorful, fancy sari. Today when she emerged from the back room, she had on a yellow sari. Kavitha squinted and thought that it might be chiffon, with a blue border of some sort. The breeze swept up her palloo as she walked from room to room. She looked like a butterfly. She looked like the petals of a flower. When the husband arrived, he had clearly brought home snacks to eat with their tea—perhaps pakora or maybe samosa, Kavitha guessed—because the young wife dashed to the kitchen and returned with a plate. Then she went back, and after a few minutes, brought out their teas on a tray. Kavitha watched them with envy. She nearly cried with it.

"Your jewels," he repeated.

The middle-aged wife and the mother of the recently departed man wept silently. It was odd, but it felt like only now, only after there was one less person in the berth, did a pall descend on the group. They moved slowly; the shadow of the train lengthened. The August heat was oppressive. Sweat trickled down their faces, their clothes stuck to their bodies. Flies entered the berth in droves but they were too scared to swat them away, to make any sudden movements. Kavitha licked her lips and tasted salt. "Hurry up," the leader said. The three other men were outside the door, standing guard, Kavitha assumed. The leader, though, watched the passengers keenly. Each of the women had left a small piece of jewelry visible, so they wouldn't suspect the ones in their shoes—Kavitha had left her earrings in, the young woman her nose ring, the middle-aged wife and the elderly mother a few bracelets. They took them off and placed them in a pile on the wooden bench. Cabbage Leaf looked at the pile, shook his head, and laughed. "I *know* you have more jewelry than that," he said. When he finished laughing, he said, "Would you like me to help you look?"

The women glanced from one to the other then they looked at the men.

Cabbage Leaf—whose name was Ahmed; Kavitha had heard one of the men guarding the door call him that—waited patiently. When no one moved, he placed his machete next to the pile, seated himself beside it, and said, "I'm going to enjoy this." Then he wrapped his arm around the waist of the young woman standing closest to him, and pulled her onto his lap. "Yes, I am," he breathed into her neck, pulling her chunni off her shoulder.

The brother of the young woman lurched forward. His mother caught the very end of his wrist but he slipped out. It didn't seem possible in such a tiny space, with so many people crowded into it, but it appeared to Kavitha as if he sailed across the berth, his arms reached out as if to strangle

Ahmed. But Ahmed was quicker. He swerved to the side, so that the brother landed in a heap against the seat. And in a flash of metal, one of the outside guards, the one with the rod, swung at the brother. All Kavitha heard was the thwack of metal against bone. The brother let out a howl, gripping his arm. Blood spurted from the wound. His mother knelt next to him, using the palloo of her sari to staunch the blood. It wouldn't stop. It was now covering the floor of the berth, pooling around their shoes.

My shoes, Kavitha thought.

"Get him out of here," Ahmed growled. "We have enough flies as it is." The guard went into the passageway and yelled for help. Another one of the guards came in, and he and the one with the metal rod dragged the brother out. He whimpered as he left the berth.

"You see what happens to heroes," Ahmed said.

Their berth was the last in the bogie, on the far end, next to the lavatories. Kavitha, seated next to the door and directly across from the little boy, caught a glimpse of the tiny steel sink that was used by the passengers to brush their teeth, and it was against this sink that the brother was propped up. Blood was still pouring out of the gash on his arm, and she wondered if he might die. She looked up, and the little boy was watching her. There was, she noticed, intention in his gaze, and she only looked away when Ahmed addressed her.

"You," the leader said, pointing to Kavitha, "give me that."

She had forgotten about her mangal sutra. She'd swapped out the gold chain of her wedding necklace for turmeric-soaked thread just before the trip, for safety's sake, but the round lockets were made of gold. How could she have forgotten? She slipped it over her head and handed it to him. Vinod seemed to wince. Was it for her or for the gold? Ahmed bounced it in his palm—the wedding necklace she'd not once taken off in ten years—up and down, up and down, as if weighing the gold. It must still hold the warmth of my skin, she thought. And then she felt a thrill, a rush of heat, flooding her body, to think that a man, any man, held in his hand the warmth of her body.

The boy was still looking at her. Kavitha couldn't understand it—his stare—but she felt too faint to return it. She hadn't eaten in over seven hours; they had emptied their water bottle three hours ago. She closed her eyes. There had been a pregnancy in Kavitha and Vinod's marriage, but the child had been stillborn. The stillbirth had been a culmination of many years of trying for children, and the next time Vinod had reached for her, an appropriate number of weeks after the failed pregnancy, she had looked at him evenly, a little sadly, and said, "Please. No more." In her memory, that was the second instance of a flicker passing across his eyes. She knew it was unfair—all of it—but she felt gratitude toward Vinod for understanding, for not having touched her since, and in a small way, he had increased, incrementally, her love for him.

When she opened her eyes, Ahmed was by the window. He was searching the bags of the older couple. The many

210 | AN UNRESTORED WOMAN

buckles and belts had been hacked off by the machete, but there were still bundles tucked under the wooden seats, and the couple and their daughter-in-law were making matters worse by their distress, by opening and reopening the same bundles and folding and refolding the same clothes. Most of these clothes were now strewn across the berth. Vinod, who was sitting next to Kavitha, reached over and patted her hand, as if to calm her, but she was already strangely calm. Even with one of the guards standing right next to her, on the other side of the door, close enough to touch, so close that his metal rod was within Kavitha's arm's reach.

When she looked again at the boy, he was looking straight back at her. This time, she slowly came to understand that he was trying to tell her something. But what? Kavitha watched him. And as she did the boy raised his right index finger to his right ear and tapped it. She stared at him. Why was he tapping his ear? Did it hurt? She turned to Vinod, but his attention was fixed on Ahmed. When Kavitha spun back, the boy was pointing toward the guard, the one who was standing by the door. What could he mean? She guessed now that he wanted her to listen, but to what? The guard was silent, unmoving. The only other sound was an occasional scream from another bogie, loud enough to travel through the train. There must be other men, in other parts of the train. She had assumed it: these four could not possibly subdue a whole train. But why would he want her to listen to *that*? She strained her ears some more. There were a few night sounds that reached her, an owl, perhaps, or a bulbul, but those were infrequent, and could hardly be the reason for the boy's signaling. She knew he wasn't deaf or mute, because she'd seen the boy and his father conversing earlier. So what was it?

Then, there was a lull. A quiet. For a few seconds, a few precious seconds, there was no screaming, no wailing, Ahmed was busy looking through a bag, and even the old couple and the daughter-in-law were restrained, stoic as they gathered their remaining tattered bags. And that was when she heard it. Footsteps. At first, they meant nothing to her. She looked at the boy, perplexed. He had heard them too, and she knew because he nodded. *They* were what he had wanted her to hear. But why? Kavitha concentrated. Footsteps. She heard them approaching, growing louder. And louder. And then, just as the footsteps passed the guard in front of their door, she arched her neck and saw that it was one of the guards who had come with Ahmed. So he was patrolling the bogie. She had assumed all three guards were standing outside their door, but now it made sense that one of them would have to patrol the passengers in the other berths.

She sat back and looked at the boy. She hardly had a chance to blink when, in the next instant, the other guard passed the one at the door, *going the other way.* She nearly gasped. *Two* of the guards were patrolling. And not only that, since theirs was the last berth in their bogie, one of the guards, at any given time, was probably in the next bogie over. He wasn't even *in* their bogie, let alone anywhere near their berth.

She had thought there were three men outside the door. But there was only one.

Kavitha had no idea what any of this meant, but she knew it meant something. She nearly reached out and hugged the boy. And he seemed to know it because he smiled.

Kavitha sat back. She held her breath. She knew there was not much time. Ahmed had already moved on to searching the bags of the younger sister and her mother. She mapped out the layout of their bogie in her head. There were eight berths, exactly like theirs, behind them. Those berths were being patrolled just as theirs was, except Ahmed had already looted the other eight berths. In front were the two doors, facing each other, that led on and off the train. Past the doors were the lavatory and the sink. And against this sink the brother still slumped. He seemed conscious, but barely. Between the lavatory and the sink area was a narrow passageway that led to the next bogie. She knew all their hope was in front, where the doors were, but that was all she knew.

She thought about the layout, and she despaired. There was no way out, not with a guard standing by the door, and two more approaching or within earshot. It would have to be lightning quick, before the two patrol guards could be alerted, but even then.

She looked at Vinod. It was growing dark outside, and all the lights in the train had been extinguished, but she could still see his face, wary of Ahmed's movements, watching him as he unpacked the suitcases of the mother and her daughter. Vinod's body was as it had always been, since the day they'd married, slim, straight-backed, the recent gray at his temples only accentuating his seriousness, his reserve. She wanted, for the first time in the ten years she'd known him, to collapse into his arms. She wanted to weep. She wanted to say, There has to be a way out. "How are you holding up?" he whispered. Instead of answering she rested her forehead against his upper arm and felt the knobbiness of his shoulder bone, its hardness against the hardness of her forehead; she felt in that moment that the answer must lie in the body, in its unquenchable will to live. Her gaze fell on the little boy's feet; they dangled off the floor of the train and his shoes hung loose around them, a size too big. The end of the piece of twine he'd put in them was visible, near his left ankle. She looked at the piece of twine and then she lifted her head.

The boy still seemed as though he was listening to the footsteps, and when he noticed her gaze, Kavitha pointed at his shoes and gestured for him to pass her its contents. The boy waited for Ahmed to turn away, just as Kavitha had hoped he would, and quickly handed her the two thin, flat pebbles and the piece of twine. There had been a chit of paper, she recalled, but this he kept for himself. Again, nothing was quite clear in her mind, but never had two rocks and a piece of twine seemed to hold so much promise. The contents of her shoes—a necklace, some rings, and a set of matching bracelets—held none.

Kavitha waited. She didn't know what she was waiting for, but she knew she had to wait.

Ahmed, in the meantime, had found the jewelry in the shoes of the young woman. Kavitha only became aware of it when he laughed out loud and said, "So *that's* where they are." He turned to face the rest of the berth. "Everybody," he said, swinging his machete, his voice rising at their collusion, "take them off."

Kavitha slowly undid the buckle of her sandals; all this time, the hem of her sari had covered them. Her necklace fell out first. Ahmed picked it up with his machete. It dangled off the tip like a lizard, like something writhing, and not meant to be touched. He added it to the pile of jewelry on the bench. Just as he turned back toward her, the old man, standing in the corner by the window, clutched at his chest. He let out a long groan and collapsed onto the seat. "Sasurji!" his daughter-in-law shrieked. His wife was bent over him, pleading, "*Kya baat hai?* What's wrong?"

"Air," someone said, "give him air."

Ahmed's face bristled. The daughter-in-law rose to take the old man outside, but Ahmed pushed her down. "Stay where you are," he seethed.

"He needs air," she pleaded, "he might die."

"You all might," Ahmed said. He summoned the guard posted at the door. "Get the old man some air," he said. "And stand where I can see you." The guard stepped into the berth and led the old man to the door. They stood just outside, in the passageway.

Kavitha counted to ten in her head. One of the guards went by. Then the other.

"I need to use the lavatory," she said.

The others were busy emptying their shoes. Ahmed took no notice of her.

"I said, I have to use the lavatory."

"Shut up."

"It's female trouble," she said.

Vinod gave her a sharp look. Ahmed paused. "Leave your shoes here," he said, the pile of jewelry rising behind him like a hill of sand.

The boy looked at Kavitha. She looked back at him.

The brother, the one slumped by the sink, lifted his eyes when she came out of the berth. The bleeding had slowed, it seemed to her, but he was clearly weak. He had gone pale; his clothes and skin were soaked with blood. For a fleeting moment, she thought she might help him, perhaps even by simply lifting him to a sitting position, but she knew there was no room for that. No time. She passed the old man, the guard, both at the window facing the berth, and when she reached the brother, she knelt swiftly next to his ear, shoved one of the pebbles into his hand (his left; the good one), and whispered, "Throw it. Throw it the moment I come out of the lavatory."

She jumped up and ducked inside. Had he heard? Was he even conscious? She listened for the footsteps of the guards. She could no longer hear them, not with the door closed, only when they were just outside the lavatory door would she be able to hear. Breathe, she told herself, taking a breath. Breathe again, she said. And she did this over and over and over again, thinking only of the little boy.

The lavatory had no window. Just a squat toilet, a tap for water, and a handle for grip. The hole was open and showed the gravel on the tracks. She looked through the hole, lined with excrement, and saw the gravel. Every stone the same color, quarried in some distant place, and varying only slightly in shape. The years following the stillbirth had been like that. She had often wondered, during those years, whether she should have named the baby. She decided it was better that she hadn't. Not because she would have felt a greater loss—there was not, she knew, a loss any greater—but because naming the child, a girl they had told her, would have been an act of bravery, and she didn't want to be brave. She wanted all the fears and weakness of a dark, unnamed place. And she wanted to love the child in that way, without hope and without a name.

When both guards had passed and been gone a few seconds, she opened the lavatory door. At the sound of the door, the brother seemed to wake as if from a deep sleep. He looked at the pebble, a little too long, a little too long, Kavitha fretted, then flung it down the corridor. Ahmed yelled, "What was that?" The guard, the one by the old man, took a few tentative steps past the berth.

This was the moment. This was it.

Kavitha darted past the brother, reached in, and grabbed the little boy's hand. They jumped from the train, through the door near the lavatory, and as soon as they hit the ground, Kavitha handed the little boy one end of the twine, shoved him against the door, and said, "Hold it. Tight." She held the other end, on the other side of the door. Ahmed came racing out, they held on until he tripped, and leapt out of the way so they wouldn't break his fall. Then they ran.

It was dark. There were a few stars, not many. The sliver of moon cast hardly any light. They scurried under the bogie, up a few cars, toward the engine, and lay on the couplings, facedown, their arms wrapped tight around them. Neither spoke. Kavitha waited until the guards had run past, checking under the bogies and inside them, then indicated the ladder that led to the roof of the train. They climbed up—the rungs digging into Kavitha's bare, bleeding feet—and crawled to the middle, if for no other reason than to be halfway in case they had to run in either direction. It was from this vantage point that Kavitha saw a road in the distance, a half mile away, at least; a thin, dark ribbon that she assumed was a road. But it was empty; not a car or a lorry or a bullock cart passed.

The night deepened.

She could not have said how much time had gone by when she saw two small lights in the distance, almost pinpricks in the night sky. They grew—slowly, because they were so far away. "There," she whispered, "look." The boy raised his head. "What do we do?" he said. They waited. The lights got bigger. Alarmingly fast. She knew there was no way for both of them to reach the road before the lights passed them. She studied the ground. Near the train was a small tree. Farther along was what looked to be a pile of luggage.

She handed the boy the second pebble.

She saw, after a time, his small, murky shape moving to the tree. Then the luggage. He had told her, before he'd descended the ladder, that he'd aimed pebbles at moving trains lots of times, in his village. "I never missed," he boasted. Kavitha didn't point out to him that the moving light was not a train, but something much smaller. She didn't tell him, But it's dark. And she didn't say, We only get to play this game once.

She heard a clink. Didn't she? What else could it be? There was nothing for many, many miles surrounding the train. That was of course why Ahmed and his men had picked this spot. And that's what she had thought while traveling on the train: that to journey through such emptiness was to invite it inside.

The light stopped.

The driver of the lorry, a burly Sikh who spoke very little, except to say, "I'm going to Attari, no further," ignored Kavitha.

"But we have to get the police," she said. "The authorities, the military, I don't know. That train is under siege," she cried. "My husband is on it, his father. People are hurt." The cabin of the lorry was dark. She turned from the driver to the boy. He was staring out of the window.

"He wasn't my father," the boy said, falling silent again.

Kavitha looked at him, as if for the first time. "What's your name?" she asked.

"Mustafa."

A Muslim. But why was he going to India? They drove on and on, eastward.

"You didn't miss," she said to Mustafa. Then she said, "Was that luggage?"

"No."

"What was it?"

"Kerosene," he said.

And she too fell silent.

They reached Attari late the next morning. She'd learned from Mustafa that the man she'd taken to be his father was a Hindu friend of his parents', entrusted to take their son to relatives living in East Pakistan. "But where are your parents?" she'd asked.

He'd looked away, and said nothing. After a moment he'd turned to her and said, "My cousins are waiting."

She knew she would take him there. He refused to take another train, and she was not keen on it, either, so they traveled slowly, overland by road. Mostly lorries and bullock carts, a passing car if they were fortunate. She had silver anklets she'd pushed up her calves, so that Ahmed wouldn't see, and she traded these for money. It ran out well before they got to East Pakistan. In the presence of other people, the two were often silent, letting them assume they were mother and son. That seemed easiest.

Sitting for these long stretches of quiet, Kavitha was surprised by how often she thought of Vinod. She knew he was gone, that she was now a widow. The awareness was not startling. Not even frightening. I was widowed long ago, she thought. And she knew that on the train, when she'd laid her head on his shoulder, and had felt the roundness and knobbiness of a bone so funny, so irreverent, so unlike him, she had said her good-bye.

They were on a horse cart, nearing East Pakistan. Maybe a day, no more. It was late afternoon. It was a covered, two-wheeled cart, and Kavitha lay in its shade, dozing. Mustafa lay beside her. The motion of the cart woke her (or was it a dream) and she said to Mustafa, "What happened to us, it's ours. Yours and mine. Don't speak of it."

And in his half sleep, perhaps also dreaming, Mustafa heard, "You are mine. Don't speak." And so he never did.

Curfew

S afia's earliest memory of her grandfather was of being on a boat with him. Or a ferry. If the rickety, inelegant, swaying raft they were on could be called a ferry. Safia was four years old. She and her grandfather were crossing the Ravi River, northwest of Lahore, and her grandfather, earlier, in a fit of something Safia could not understand, decided to take her on a river excursion. The two sat in one corner of the raft; when Safia looked down she could see the brown of the water between the wooden slats. Every now and then, a small twig or a discarded wrapper would float by and Safia would try to squeeze her tiny hand through the slats to reach for it, but her grandfather slapped her arm away every time. Safia looked around. Also piled onto the raft were a motorbike, numerous bicycles, and bushel after bushel of vegetables, belonging to vendors going back to their homes after coming to Lahore to sell their wares. There was also a watermelon in the middle of the raft. From what Safia could tell, it was positioned in the exact center of it, almost as if the watermelon was the talisman keeping the raft afloat.

Safia studied the faces of the other occupants. There was another child, but only a baby, and it was crying while the mother tried to shush it by pointing out the river and the tiny island of silt rising out of it and the far shore. Why would a baby be interested in any of that? Safia wondered. Then she looked at the vendors, each in turn; they all looked miserable. They clung to their bushel of vegetables as if they would be lost without them, as if they had left behind, on the retreating shore, all doubt as to what they loved most in the world. The oarsman, a dark man, short but muscular, maneuvered across the current with a long pole, lifting and pushing, lifting and pushing. He looked like a nice man but mostly he looked bored. Safia turned away and climbed onto her grandfather's lap. She reached her hand into the pocket of her grandfather's kurta and felt something. She pulled it out. It was a pebble, round and black and shiny. Pretty. "Is this yours?" Safia asked.

Her grandfather nodded.

Safia stared at it some more then she licked it. She liked how it felt against her tongue, cool and rough, salty even. "Can I have it?"

Her grandfather—his gray beard long enough to curl in the breeze—shook his head no.

"But why?"

Just then, just as Safia was shifting it from one hand to the other, the pebble slipped away and plopped between the slats into the water. Safia gasped. She bent her head all the way down to the opening between the boards and watched the pebble disappear. It sank so fast it was as if a hand had snatched it and pulled it down. She waited for it to come back up, but it never did. When she looked up again they were nearing the shore, and when she looked again at her grandfather, there were tears in his eyes.

Her family had warned her. Her mother, when Safia had turned twenty-five and had announced she was marrying Ethan, shook her head and said, "Grief. It will only come to grief." Even her ailing grandfather—who'd moved to London to live with them only a year ago—sighed loudly and Safia could've sworn he mumbled the word *fool* under his breath. She swung around in amazement to look at him but he was looking away, out of the garden window.

Grief, grief, grief, Safia chanted softly.

She and Ethan were waiting in a square called Piazza della Passera. It was quaint, cobblestoned, with an island of trees at its center and restaurants along its edges. Patio umbrellas clustered over groups of two and three and four, laughing and toasting and eating, the evening sky peeking through the gaps among the umbrellas.

Safia closed her eyes. She saw the pebble again, disappearing into the water. "I feel like a pebble," she said aloud.

Ethan gave her a look of incomprehension; his eyes

squinted and he opened his mouth, but then he corrected it into a strained smile, as if he'd reminded himself—as he seemed to be doing every few minutes—that they were in Florence, that they were on holiday, and what a joy it was: to be here with his wife on their third anniversary. The strongest number, he'd mentioned, as they were packing. "You can't knock over something with three legs," he'd said. Yes, she hoped it was true, the bit about the three legs.

"It won't be long now," he said cheerily. "We've been here over an hour." Safia passed her gaze over the diners. Most of them were chattering away in Italian. There were a few American couples, and one group of Germans. They were the only mixed couple. She noted that, and then she turned away from the diners. A little light remained in the sky, but that too soon crumbled. The hostess, a lithe Italian woman with curly hair, brushed past them.

Safia heard approaching laughter, and when she looked across the square, a cadre of young men was crossing it. They seemed about the same age as them, Safia and Ethan, hardly much younger, but they walked and laughed with such ease, such brazenness. She steadied her voice, told herself she couldn't scream, that she wouldn't. "Oxford, do you think, or Cambridge?" she asked.

Ethan, who'd been reading the menu for the past ten minutes, whipped around to look at her. "How do mean?"

"Where do you think she would've gone? Oxford or Cambridge?"

Ethan's eyes widened then narrowed. He was quiet. Safia thought how very different he was just a few months ago. Before Minoo died. His eyes, back then, would not have blazed so blue. They would've been serene, like sea glass, and he would've winked and said, "Harvard, you goose."

But now, after a long moment—during which it seemed to Safia that all the voices and clinking and laughter in the square died, as if a curtain were lifted and a sudden hush had fallen over an audience—did he say, softly, "Safia, she's gone. She's gone."

Her eyes grew warm. She wished he hadn't said them so softly, those words, she wished he had screamed them. Their softness made them so true. "I'm just asking, is all," she managed to say. It wasn't long before the hostess motioned for them to follow her and led them to a table on the outer ring of the umbrellas. Ethan seated himself with a sigh. He looked at her and fiddled with a fork that was set on a white folded napkin. "We can get through this," he said. Safia nodded. She tried to smile. It was just like him these days to say such a thing. To say something so bland, so thin, so rustic. And so utterly untrue.

Grief, she repeated to herself.

Ethan ordered melanzane alla parmigiana, insalata caprese, a plate of pasta stuffed with taleggio cheese and pear, and a bottle of Chianti. The waiter said, *"Perfetto, signore. Mille grazie,*" and went away. There was a little boy at another table, fussing and dropping spoons. Safia tried hard not to look at him. She could see the mother, bending to pick them up, losing her patience. She turned away.

The wine arrived. It was poured into two of those squat glasses they used on the Continent, as if to say they were past the stem, past all the secrets of wine, and into its wild and crimson heart. Ethan raised his glass. "To us," he said. Safia smiled and looked through the gap in the umbrellas. None of it was even his fault (was it?), but she could hardly look at him. Even with her eyes closed she could see the striations on his neck, the reddish blond hair spiking out of his skin like desert thorns, weeds that you pluck and pluck against a dry desert sky and they spring up again and again as though they had a will of their own, a will so endless and untamed she thought it might choke her in the night.

"Your granddad Mustafa," he was saying, holding his glass against the lantern on the table. "Eight, did you say?"

"Nine."

He let out a low whistle. "Imagine. Nine," Ethan said, his voice rising with interest.

Safia thought of Minoo. Lying there in her crib, the day before she'd died, as if for all the world she would learn to walk, and to talk, and to whirl through life with the same laughter and glory that was in this square, and that she would be protected, always, as if by these umbrellas.

"Not a word?"

Safia shook her head. She took a sip of her wine. Her grandfather's story was something of family lore, gathered in bits and pieces: he'd been on a train, crossing from Pakistan into India. He was already an orphan, his parents having been killed by a Hindu mob months earlier. And as if that were not enough, the train he was on had been looted then torched. He had been the only person to survive, and had not spoken a word since.

The insalata arrived. Ethan heaped the mozzarella and cubes of tomato onto his plate. The olive oil, in the lantern light, slipped and glowed like gold. Safia thought of him—she thought of his efficiency. It was terrifying, it was maddening, this efficiency of his. At the hospital, afterward, he'd been the one to call both sets of parents, to call work, to call the mortuary, to call, call, call. Safia had watched him. At first she hadn't understood, she couldn't even *hear*, and so she'd asked him, "Who are you calling?" She didn't hear his response but she remembered searching her mind. So suddenly airy and weightless. Who was there to call? Her baby daughter was dead. Who should she call? All of that hospital, all of London was empty. All the world, really. She could pass a hand through the steel and concrete pillars in the waiting room of the hospital, she could topple with a flick of her fingers the coarse, useless bodies, bloated with life that squirmed past her. Call? On their way out of the hospital they passed the chapel and she said aloud, into the dim of its open door, "You? Not you. *You* died when she did."

Two years after Safia's excursion on the ferry with her grandfather, she and her parents moved to London from Lahore. They moved in with an uncle who lived in Croydon, and Safia started school at the Coloma Convent Girls' School. She didn't know more than three words of English when she arrived but by the end of the year she had forgotten nearly all her Urdu, having replaced it with a gleaming new language that she tossed around as easily as a ball. "Do you want to go back to Lahore?" her mother asked her toward the end of their second year. Safia knew why she was asking: her father was nearly finished with his graduate degree and in order to remain in England he'd have to apply for a post-study work visa. Otherwise they'd have to return to Lahore. She'd heard her mother and father talking deep into the night about whether to stay or go. The money was better, of course, and life was easier in London, but occasionally her mother would whisper, with a small and plaintive voice, "But Jannu, Lahore is home."

It had been raining all morning, but by the time her mother posed the question to Safia it had stopped, though the clouds still clung low and dark. Safia was watching Noddy and Big Ears on television. Her mother pulled her onto her lap, but Safia continued watching, peeking at the screen through her mother's sheer chunni. She brushed a strand of hair from Safia's face; her fingers smelled of garlic and mutton and ghee, and faintly sweet like cinnamon. "What do you think?" she asked. "Do you want to go back to Lahore?" Safia lowered her head and pretended to think. She concentrated on the voices coming from the television, and tried to recall all the things she remembered about Lahore. She saw the peepal tree in their old garden, and she remembered that her socks used to slip down her calves during morning exercises. The teacher had once rapped her on the wrist with a ruler for stopping to pull them up. She remembered her grandfather, the rickety old ferry, and the strangeness of that day. She remembered the distant shore that couldn't even keep a baby from crying, let alone her grandfather. "I want to stay," she finally said and knew immediately that it was the wrong answer: her mother's face swung as dark and low as the clouds, and even at that age—even at the age when every beginning has a rightness to it—Safia knew *this* was the wrong way to begin.

Maybe it was the white of his skin that disgusted her.

She leaned in to have a closer look. My god, why had she never noticed? That field of pink pores, grotesque how they swayed and shivered like jelly when he chewed. Like uncooked flesh. Uncooked flesh: that was the true horror. That it was unfinished, unmade. Sitting on a counter. The white like runny tapioca, like maggots.

Ethan looked at her. "Why aren't you eating?"

She took a bite. She swallowed it. He'd proposed this trip to Italy and when she'd asked him why, he'd said, "I'm concerned."

"Concerned?"

"Wouldn't you be? All you do is sit in the flat. You don't go out, you don't pick up the phone. Do you even eat?"

"Do you think it's right," she asked him after a few bites, "that we lost a child before the third leg?"

It took him a moment to understand but she knew he did when he wrapped his hand into a slow fist. Safia put down her fork. She thought then that she should take it, his hand, his fist, and kiss every knuckle. Move over those mountainous stretches of skin—white and taut with rage—her lips lingering, breathing in what was left, what might be salvaged. But she only sat there, looking at it. She had no arms to reach out. No lips with which to kiss. And that rage: she felt it too.

They stayed. Safia and her parents moved into their own flat in New Malden and her father took a job as a chemist for a pharmaceutical company. Her mother stayed at home. Safia changed schools, and changed once again when her father took up the post as head chemist at a company in Twickenham. Safia was barely aware of her parents; she spent most of her time reading *Anna Karenina*, staring out of schoolroom windows, and wondering what it would be like to kiss Count Vronsky.

On her sixteenth birthday Safia and one of her classmates snuck out and went dancing at an underage club in London

Bridge. One of the boys on the dance floor—some boy who'd been watching them all night and looked West African, the thick lips, the piercing white eyes against the dark of his skin, who made Safia think that the race of men would continue on and on, that death was no match against the beauty of such men—leaned down and said, "Follow me."

She did. He led her to a small room next to the loo. He edged her against the wall, with its dull pink wallpaper stained and peeling against her back. Then he kissed her. Just like that. As if she'd asked him to. He smiled and said, "You're cute. But that friend of yours, the blondie, now she's a stunner."

Safia stared up at him.

"Think you could get her over here?"

She yanked her arm away from him. "*Khusra*," she yelled into his face. She smiled faintly; so she remembered some Urdu, after all.

"What?" he said. "I said you were cute, didn't I?"

She pushed past him and through the line of people waiting for the loo. "Eh, eh," he yelled after her, "you Paki slag. What's got into you?"

Safia looked back. The bright of his eyes still shone through the crowd of people, but then someone passed in front of him and she was sucked again into the mass of bodies, and in that moment she had a strange and unsettling intimation. A trace of something she'd always sensed, of something her mother had long ago said, and of a thing that that African boy knew: that she wasn't home. That home wasn't Lahore, and that it wasn't London. Not really. And that home had never been a thing she'd found. It was a thing she'd lost.

It was eleven o'clock. The melanzane hadn't yet arrived. Ethan looked at his watch. "You think we'll make it?"

Safia took a sip of her wine. They were staying at a monastery in the Oltrarno. "It's architecturally significant, Safia. You should appreciate that. From the time of the Medicis," Ethan had insisted. And it was charming: the narrow streets, the artisan shops, well away from the tourists and crowds north of the Arno. Florence, too, delighted her. She wandered the churches, the Duomo, stood in front of the religious paintings at the Uffizi, and tried to find a single piece of art that didn't derive its beauty from suffering. The suffering of a mother, mainly. She couldn't. The monastery itself was full of Renaissance-era frescoes, and there was the pleasure, unexpected and lovely, of being woken from a nap by evening vespers. And though it had a nightly curfew, midnight, they'd reasoned—searching the Internet a month ago in their London flat—that it would hardly be a problem getting back before such a late hour. The waiter, whom Ethan tried to summon, was busy seating a group of six at a table next to theirs. "What an hour to *begin* eating," he said with wonder.

Safia looked through the umbrellas at the stars.

Maybe it was punishment. Maybe people of different races weren't meant to marry. Maybe their babies died. The thought made sense, in a way. We'd roamed away from each other all those hundreds of thousands of years ago; there must've been a reason. There must've been an explanation. But it was ridiculous, of course; she had loads of friends who'd married out of race and had had beautiful healthy babies who cooed and gurgled and woke up in the mornings.

Had *she* done something wrong? Her mother had been so ashamed she hadn't told anyone of her engagement to Ethan for three months. Her father hadn't spoken to her for two. Her grandfather had blinked, and looked away. But that had been years ago, before the wedding. And back then she'd been young; she'd thought weathering something was like passing a moment, like waiting in a rain. Eventually, sooner or later, you knew you'd find yourself inside, by a warm fire, in dry clothes. Now she knew better: weathering was a thing that had nothing to do with rain and nothing to do with fire. It was you, anywhere—in warmth, in rain, on a ferry on the Ravi, in a square in Florence—it was you, everywhere, in all the palaces of the world, broken.

She left secondary school and studied architecture at London South Bank, doing moderately well but without the zeal of her fellow students. After graduation she landed an internship with a small architectural firm in Kings Cross and moved into a flat with two other women. Within the first week at her new job she was restless. "All I do is design the bloody boil-in-bag aisle at Marks and Spencer," she complained to one of her roommates, Tabitha, "and even that as an *assistant*. The team leader said to me today, *actually said to me*, Tab, he said, 'Safia, you're not taking boil-in-bag very seriously, are you?' What does he want me to do? Shag one? That's what I should do. Design an aisle for shag-a-bag." Safia was drunk, and her team leader was Ethan. Within a year they'd secretly moved in together—on the other side of London from Safia's parents and without telling them—and Safia had left the firm to pursue a course in art history. But that too came to nothing and by the time they were married Ethan was telling his friends and family that Safia was "exploring her options."

But Safia was doing nothing of the sort. She wasn't exploring; she was waiting. And though she wasn't sure what she was waiting for, she decided that waiting, even when it had no clear end, was a fine way to spend one's time. It even held a certain inexplicable charm. Then her waiting was over: a year and a half after they were married Safia was pregnant.

Ethan wiped up the last bits of melanzane with bread. It was forty minutes till midnight. Safia thought for a moment that it might be nice not making it back by curfew. They'd have to sleep in one of the squares. Or on a bench along the Arno. Maybe even huddled under one of the trees in the Boboli Gardens. But somewhere without a roof. That was the part that most delighted her. She pictured it: the soft summer breeze, the thick blanket of stars, the scent of water. She'd never slept in such a place and it beckoned her in the way

Minoo's cries had beckoned her: with a thrill, a rush of sorrow, concern, and such a sudden and electric feeling of life that the hair on her arms stood on end.

A young couple walked past them, eating gelato.

"I think she would've preferred it," Safia said, "to ice cream, I mean. What do you think?"

Ethan began to speak but then seemed to change his mind. It was so like him these days, Safia thought. Talking and talking but then silencing himself when something so needed to be said. It mattered, didn't it? Whether she would've liked ice cream or gelato, whether she would've gone to Oxford or Cambridge.

The pasta arrived. When Ethan cut open a ravioli the thick milky taleggio oozed out like sea foam, studded with glistening shavings of pear. He took a bite. "Saf, you gotta try this," he said, holding up a forkful.

She looked at him. His thick fingers, the dripping pasta, the cold of the metal. What would it feel like—that fork—scraping against her neck, her wrist, her heart. And that knife, the ones the Italians were using to cut their steaks, what would that feel like gliding along the inside of her thigh. It would make a line; she could draw a map. And *that* would be the true country. Not this one, and not the one she lived in, and not the one she'd left.

"I think I'll just have some coffee," she said. He nodded, looked at his watch. They had twenty minutes left.

* * *

Safia looked through the gap in the umbrellas. The stars spun. They rattled in the sky like bones.

Ethan paid the bill and looked again at his watch. "Safia, we've gotta go," he said, springing from his chair. "Now!"

They dashed out of the Piazza della Passera. Down the Via Maggio. Across the church of Santo Spirito. The narrow streets and alleys rang with their footsteps. She'd occasionally spy a lighted square at the end of a side alley, or the sounds of a television streaming out of an open window, but mostly the streets were deserted. And for all the world they were the only ones left in it.

Ethan was in front of her. "I know a shortcut," he said.

They ducked under a stone gate. She caught a glimpse of a chubby gargoyle above her head, its tongue sticking out and laughing. The face of a baby. "Minoo," she whispered under her breath, "why'd you have to leave so soon?"

"What did you say?" Ethan called back.

"I said, how long?"

"A minute or two, at most."

They strode faster. Safia was nearly running to keep up. Her feet pounded cobblestone; the soles of her shoes felt as flimsy as paper. The roar traveled up her legs, burst across her back like a scream. Her body, her body, her oh so lonesome body ceased. She ceased. And all that existed was her stone, her feet, her flight. That West African boy had been right: her friend's straw-colored hair, its glint of gold, was the light of the world. But she—she and he—*they* were the dark beyond. They were the universe, entire.

Ethan, turning a corner, was a blur. A few steps in front. He said something over his shoulder. What was it? Just two words—and she asked him to repeat them because they were true, they were the only truth left in the world.

"I said, ice cream," he said, taking in deep mouthfuls of air. "I think she would've preferred ice cream."

The tears streamed down Safia's face. She nearly laughed.

Why? Why a pebble, why a baby, why a distant shore? Why did they all have to disappear into a brown and murky depth?

There was no answer.

There were only those two words. And they held her as if in an embrace.

Ethan's arm swung back and she knew that soon, one day soon, she would take it. Take it, hold it, pull him to her and say, Enough. This moment is enough. How young we are. How old our sorrow. I want to wake. I want to wake as lovers are meant to wake. And this grief: this grief we must leave. Leave in one of the many airports we will pass, maybe a train station in the Alps, a bus depot in Rome. Leave, because it is not meant for us. Leave, before it has a name. Before we give it room. Before we seat it, like a friend, at our table.

"There," Ethan said, pointing to the monastery. But it was on the other side of the long square. The lights had been turned off. The dim of the doorway narrowed. "Run!" he shouted.

And so she ran.

Her old grandfather: sitting alone, quiet all of these years, in a London flat. She understood now. She saw him: a boy of nine, alone in the world. He'd begun again. Maybe she could too.

She sprinted faster. She could no longer feel her feet. Only her breath was left. Deep, pulsing with the power of kings. We leave. We leave the places we're born, the places we're meant to die, and we wander into the world as defenseless as children. Against such wilderness, such desert.

The warm night air cradled her, lifted her up. There was someone at the door; Ethan waved frantically. How long the journey, she thought. How far away that abode of peace. And yes, its doors may close. Its lights may dim. And it may not even be for us to enter. But this, Safia thought—running and running and running—*this* is how you begin.

GLOSSARY

aam: mango

almirah: wardrobe, cabinet

amchur: a tangy mango-based powder

anna: former monetary unit of India and Pakistan, equal to 1/16 of a rupee

ayananta: solstice

beedi: a thin, cheap cigarette popular in India

beti: girl

bhai: brother, friend

bhelpuri: a savory snack food made by combining puffed rice with other ingredients

biryani: an Indian dish made with highly seasoned rice and meat, fish, or vegetables

Brahmachari: bachelor

Brahmaputra: a trans-boundary river flowing through northeastern India

brahmin: a member of the highest caste in Hinduism, traditionally a priest

burqa: outer garment worn by women in some Islamic traditions

chai: spiced tea

chal: move

chappals: sandals or slippers

chikoo: tropical fruit

choot or chutia: a derogatory term for vagina, used to refer to a
fool or useless person

chota: small or younger

chowkidar: security guard

chunni: a long piece of cloth that hangs over the shoulders to cover
a woman's chest, usually worn over a long tunic or shalwar

dal: a common lentil stew

darajin: seamstress

dhoti: traditional men's garment wrapped around the waist and
legs, knotted at the waist

Ganesh: elephant-headed god in Hinduism

Ganga or Ganges: a trans-boundary river that flows through India
and Bangladesh, considered sacred by Hindus

ghee: clarified butter

Gomti: a tributary of the Ganges River that flows through Uttar
Pradesh

goonda: hired thug

gulabi: pink

gur: a brown, unrefined sugar

Hooghly: a distributary of the Ganges River that flows through
West Bengal

ji: added to show respect at the end of a name, can be used alone
but is most often a suffix

jilebi: a chewy sweet made from deep-fried batter soaked in sugar
syrup

kaffir: derogatory term for a black African

katwa: derogatory term for a Muslim man

kheer: rice pudding

khusra: eunuch

kumkum: red powder used to adorn the images of deities; also used for the red dot placed in the center of the forehead, generally indicating a married or marriageable woman

kurta: traditional form of upper garment worn by men and women

kya baat hai?: What is the matter?

Laddu or laddoo: ball-shaped sweets, usually made from flour, coconut, or semolina

lassi: a yogurt-based drink, served sweet or salty

lehenga: a long flowing skirt worn by young women and girls

lungi: a kind of sarong worn by men in parts of South Asia

machher jhol: Bengali spicy fish stew

malik: tribal chieftain or local aristocrat

mangal sutra: a sacred necklace that a groom ties around a bride's neck; it is rarely taken off

memsahib or memsab: term used in colonial times to refer to a upper-class white woman; now used to refer to any upper-class woman

moorkh: idiot

nahi: no

nakaam: worthless or useless

nanaji: maternal grandfather

nimbu pani: lemonade

pagal: crazy person

paisa: unit of currency, equal to 1/100 of a rupee

pakora: a snack food made by dipping various vegetables in chickpea flour batter and frying them in oil

palloo: the free end of the sari, usually draped over the shoulder

paneer: a fresh cheese common in South Asian cuisine

papad: a thin, fried disc made of lentils, generally, and served as an accompaniment to a meal

paratha: a layered flatbread, sometimes stuffed with vegetables or meat

pulao: a rice dish, similar to pilaf

punkah: fan; in colonial times, it was affixed to the ceiling and pulled by hand

puri: deep-fried bread made of wheat flour

randi: prostitute

Ravi: trans-boundary river flowing through northwest India and eastern Pakistan, eventually draining into the Indus River in Pakistan

rossogolla: dessert made of white spongy cheese balls suspended in sugar syrup

roti: flatbread made from wheat flour

rupee: unit of currency

Sabarmati: a river in Gujrat, in western India

sadhu: Hindu mystic, sage

safaiwala: laborer

sahib: term used in colonial times to refer to an upper-class white man; now used to refer to any upper-class man

samosa: fried pastry filled with spiced potato or meat

sari: traditional dress that is wrapped around the waist and draped over the shoulder

sasurji: father-in-law

shalwar kameez: traditional dress featuring a long tunic over loose-fitting pants

subzi: curry

tehsil: a unit of government in India and Pakistan equal to a county

topee: hat

uptan: paste made out of natural ingredients, often turmeric and rosewater, applied to the bride's face and body as part of the pre-wedding beautification ritual

wallah: used as a suffix, indicating the activity in which the person is engaged

ACKNOWLEDGMENTS

I am deeply indebted to Ritu Menon and Kamla Bhasin's *Borders and Boundaries: Women in India's Partition.* My gratitude to Sandra Dijkstra and Elise Capron for their unstinting belief in me, along with Michael Krasny, for that first flight. My utmost thanks to my editor, Amy Einhorn, for making this journey possible. Caroline Bleeke has been a thoughtful guide and editor. I am also grateful to Liz Keenan and Marlena Bittner, and everyone at Flatiron Books, for their support and encouragement.

My sincerest thanks to dear friends and early readers of this collection: Jared Roehrig, Nate Waggoner, Joel Young, Matt Heitland, and to my teachers, Peter Orner and Nona Caspers, along with the entire Creative Writing Department at San Francisco State University. Over the years, Joy Viveros has been a rare and luminous friend and mentor. I am also grateful to the Elizabeth George Foundation, Nimrod International Journal, and of course to Chris Abani. Thank you for believing in me. As for Hedgebrook, Amy

Wheeler and all the people who make that beautiful place possible, my time spent there was truly the beginning of all things.

Over the years, innumerable friends have lent their support and many kindnesses. Among them, Maya Vasudevan, Zakia Afrin, Melissa Passafiume, Adam Bad Wound, Emily Doskow, Luan Stauss, Vandana Sharma, Ian Valvona, and Natalie Nevard. Tom Doskow has been an invaluable friend. Donald Tibbs, Deborah Costela, and Philip Schultz have buoyed me in times of storm. I would also like to thank Leigh Ann Morlock. Sierra Golden has been a trusted reader and friend. And, of course, my heartfelt thank-you to Meredith May. I was never alone in the darkest of woods.

My gratitude, also, to my family: Sridevi, Venkat, Siriveena, and Samanthaka Nandam. As well as Bhagya and Ramarao Inguva. And finally, this book could not have been written without Srinivas: I asked for a small, lighted corner of the world—you gave me a blazing universe.

CPSIA information can be obtained
at www.ICGtesting.com
Printed in the USA
LVHW111925100920
665418LV00008B/8